I0676719

About the Author

*Martin Roy Mortimer is a Cultural Anthropologist, having graduated
with honours for field work
performed through the
University of Newcastle in Australia.
A former high school teacher, he now resides in
the NSW Riverina district and has plans
to continue writing and publishing
science fiction into the future.
Watch for his next book!*

Novels by this author:

Suspended Earth
Starlight
Dance of Nevermind
Shades of Farthrow
Armada's Disciple
Longarm Severed
The Cinder Chronicles - Flame Rangers
The Cinder Chronicles - Ice Rangers
The Cinder Chronicles - Sand Rangers

Short story collection by this author:

When History Fractures, Heroes Rise

These and more still to come!

Visit www.suspendedearth.com
for information about other book releases.

Finding Horses

M.R. Mortimer

Maia's Adventure Down The Mountain

First published 2023

ISBN: 978-0-6482320-8-7

For Elijah

Chapter 1 – Uncle

The long shadows of the peaks crept across the afternoon, leaving darkness where the sun so briefly had cast its light. Here in the mountains, Maia grew up with the long shadows. The peaks which surrounded the village sheltered them from the outside world just as they shortened the day.

"Come, Artemis," Maia called as the young white dog trotted beside her. "Uncle will be waiting."

The dog, barely more than a puppy, did not respond other than to obey its master. It walked beside her, as tall as her knees. One day it would join the team which pulled her father's cart to market in the town down the mountains. Together, they made their way to the high end of the village, where Uncle's house stood, an end piece to the long avenue of trees which began at the central square.

Artemis glanced up at her master, watching for any further instructions. The pup's short coat rippled with the muscles beneath, an effect which led to Maia giving it the name of the goddess of the hunt. Most of the dogs had longer fur, but sometimes, there would be a short coat dog in a litter, and Maia always felt a fondness for those.

The shade enclosed her as she walked between the trees of the long avenue to Uncle's house. Maia did not mind, she was well accustomed to finding her way in darkness.

Before long, she reached the house, and entered without knocking.

"Uncle," she called out. "Sorry I'm late. Father needed my help."

"That's fine," came the deep baritone reply. "I'm in the library."

Taking a detour through the kitchen, Maia fetched a piece of dried meat for Artemis, and let her out into the small courtyard behind the house where Uncle did his laundry. She paused to tidy her long brown hair, then went to find her mentor in the Library.

"Oh, there you are," said the wizened looking man, just entering into the later half of his fifties. "Nothing too worrisome, I hope?"

"No. Father needed my help with some preparations for the fire season."

Uncle waved her into the room. His ginger beard was tinged with grey, but his pale blue eyes still sparkled with the light of a much younger man. He waved her to a desk, where the music device and some sheets of paper were already laid out for her.

"I don't have any important tasks for you today, so select some music from the device and note your thoughts. I want to know what you understand of those songs, and what you hear which no longer applies to this world."

"Yes, Uncle," Maia said, and sat on the small stool by the desk, picking up the ancient device.

She turned it over in her hands, marvelling, not for the first time, at the size of the thing. It fit comfortably in her hands, thin enough to slip into a pocket, and yet Uncle had stored on it many thousands of songs from the old times. On the back, was a small image, which looked like a piece of fruit, and from the end extended a chord, running to two small buds which she placed in her ears, as Uncle had taught her.

Maia set the device to "shuffle" and waited for the music to begin. It was like a wonderful game of chance. She had no way of knowing what music the device would select for her. Sometimes it was melodic and beautiful, others it was raucus and harsh. Some of those aggressive sounding tunes appealed to her, but others she did not enjoy at all. She often wondered what had prompted the people of the old times to create such a thing.

Today, it played a new song, one she had not heard before, and the words were strange. She changed the device settings to repeat the tune, listening carefully to the words as the man, long dead, sang as if only to her.

Maia took a few notes in her own shorthand, to remember the words she could not understand, to ask Uncle about later. The tune came to an end, and she let it start again. Soon, it repeated a fourth time, and Uncle approached her.

"You've let that song go a few times in a row. What is it?"

She held the device out, so he could see the little screen on the front.

"Tenterfield Saddler, Peter Allen. Yes, a beautiful song."

She took the buds out of her ears and smiled, humming the melody and carefully placing the device on the desk as she faced Uncle.

"You know this song?" she asked. "I quite like it, though some of the words I don't understand."

"It is a beautiful song about the way life changes a man, and the way a man changes life." Uncle said.

"What do you mean?" Maia asked.

"I mean, the song tells us a lot about a person who lived a particular life, and lived it well, and how that life changed him, and it's effect on the people around him."

"I see," Maia said, with a slight frown.

"What did you think?" Uncle asked.

"It has some nice thoughts in it. Like, the idea that time is a traveller. I get that. It's very deep. But..." she trailed off, thinking.

"But what?" Uncle prompted.

"But what is a tenterfield, and what does it mean to saddle one?"

Uncle burst into laughter, causing Maia to blush deep crimson, embarrassed that she had clearly made an error.

"You misunderstand, child," Uncle said. "Tenterfield was a place. The saddler is the man, George, who the song was about. Saddler was his job. He lived in that place, so he was the Tenterfield Saddler. Do you understand now?"

"A little, but Uncle," Maia said, looking around, feeling she was stupid for not already knowing the answers to her questions. "What is a saddler? What did the man do?"

"He made saddles, to go on horses. That's why the song talks about a jackaroo."

"OK, that makes it even more confusing," Maia said. "I don't know what a saddle is, I've no idea about horses, and as for Jackaroo..."

"Don't fret, Maia," Uncle said. "This is exactly why I have you listen to these songs. Because now I know that these are things being forgotten in today's world. Just as the rest of the village does not have the electricity to power these old devices, many other things have been lost to us since the end of the old times. Indeed, one day my panels will fail, and I will lose the ability to even keep these few devices running. That's why I long to collect as many books from those days as I can, so this village will always have this store of knowledge."

"I get that," Maia said, she was used to Uncle's speeches about the old times. "but what about the song?"

"Of course," Uncle said. "Sorry, I get off track sometimes, I know. Now, where were we? Oh yes, Tenterfield was a place."

"You said that bit."

"Oh, did I?" Uncle said, scratching his beard. "Well, the man was from there, and he worked as a saddler. He made saddles, which are like a seat thing you sit on, which goes on a horse's back."

"What are horses?" Maia asked, aching to get to the point.

"They were enormous animals, much bigger than the dogs, or the birds. In the old times, there were all kinds of animals we never see today. Horses were one beautiful example. They stood as tall as a man, on four legs, and were able to pull heavy weights, or run fast. They'd pull that cart of your father's far easier than those poor dogs he works."

"And Jackaroo?" Maia asked.

"That was a name for the people in one country, who worked on farms riding horses."

"They worked riding horses? Whatever for?"

"The horses were bigger and faster than people, so they could pull weights, heard cattle, which was a meat animal equal in size to the horse, so the Jackaroos would ride a horse so that they could keep up and be seen by the animals, you know, moving them from pasture to pasture, that sort of thing."

"Are there no horses left?" Maia asked.

"There may be," Uncle said, "But I've not seen one in many years. There are certainly none in the mountains. I have some pictures, just a minute."

The old man fetched another device, one with a larger screen and a large array of buttons at the bottom. It folded so the buttons and screen were hidden. Maia recalled him telling her it was called a laptop computer.

"I think I have some life in the battery still," Uncle said as he opened it and pressed a button near the screen.

The device beeped, and started to make a whirring sound, as things flashed up on the screen. Maia watched intently. The

4

devices were truly fascinating.

"It'll take a moment to load up, but I think I had some images on this one I can show you."

Uncle manipulated the device for several minutes, while Maia watched, until finally the screen was filled with a picture of a creature. Maia gasped.

"It's beautiful," she said. "I wish I could meet one one day."

"You never know," Uncle replied. "There could well be horses out there somewhere."

"If there are, I'll find them!" Maia said, suddenly energised by the thought. "I'll bring them home to help with work here."

"One day, perhaps," Uncle said. "I look forward to seeing you ride one home to the village. But Horses were never really used to herd chickens."

"They could pull a bigger cart than the dogs though," Maia said. "And that would make things easier for my dad."

"Perhaps it would indeed," Uncle replied. "Those dogs weren't bred for the cart work. That's why he takes it so easy and is so slow getting down the mountains. There were breeds for that kind of work, but those white shepherds weren't one of them."

"They're big and strong though."

"Yes, they are, but the work takes it's toll. You know why he refuses to work them until they're two?"

"Why?"

"Because before that their bones aren't mature enough for the strain. Remember little Artemis's grandmother? What was her name?"

"Phyllis? I was little when she died," Maia said.

"Yeah, Good old Phyllis. Poor thing had so much pain. She was always keen to work, always full of life and energy. As a pup she was too active. As an older dog, she was riddled with pain. The joints, you see. Those poor dogs suffer all to much from it if things go wrong."

"Then I'll definitely bring home horses one day!"

"I'm sure if they're out there, you'll do just that."

Uncle walked away, and began tinkering with some found object on his work bench. Maia sat imagining what it would be like to have horses in the village. Uncle had left the picture up on the folding device, and she operated the controls to look through the millions of pictures stored on it, looking for more images of horses and the people who rode them.

*   *   *

It was late when Maia returned home, and her mother was already preparing to serve the evening meal.

"Maia, you should have been home sooner. I could have used your help."

"Sorry, Mother," Maia replied, rushing to set the table as her father entered the room.

"Don't be hard on the girl, Helen," he said. "It was as much my fault as anyone's. I had her helping me before she went to Uncle's."

"That foolish old man lives in the past," Helen snapped. "Maia, I wish you'd stop spending time learning useless things and spend more time doing the things we need to keep the village going."

"He's not foolish!" Maia snapped back, then regretted it, softening her tone and looking down. "I'm sorry, Mother."

"Don't you talk back at me!" Helen said.

"Now Helen," Maia's father said. "I said don't be hard on the girl."

"But Frank!" Helen replied. "She spends all her time up there looking at that worthless junk of his, learning about things she'll never see for herself. It's pointless!"

"We need historians," Frank replied calmly. "And Uncle will not always be here to give us an insight into the past."

"But it's the past!"

"And a window to the future. You think we'd have the water infrastructure he designed without his stuff from the past? We'd be thirsty through the fire season if not for that! And I'd never have been able to make the new harnesses for the dogs without his library. If Maia want's to work with Uncle, there are far worse things she could be doing with her time."

"I guess so," Helen said. "I'm just not comfortable with our daughter spending all that time with an old man, when she could be finding herself a young one."

"In this village?" Maia snarled. "Have you seen them?"

"Maia!" her mother snapped.

"That's it, girl," Frank said, laughing. "Keep your standards high, and your value higher. No boy will step up to better himself if he's just allowed to get away with being less than he can be. I'm sure young David down the road wouldn't be so keen to impress the girls if they just took him as he was."

"That David's a gadabout," Helen said.

"Something we agree on," Maia replied. "He doesn't take anything seriously, or anyone. He'd have every girl for a night and none for a lifetime, that boy. And he's the only one my age."

"The girl has a point there, Helen," Frank said. "When they're a little older, things will change, but at her age, a year is an eternity. Don't you remember?"

"Oh Frank," Helen said, smiling and looking at him with affection. "I remember being eighteen. We were just like them, weren't we?"

The situation with her mother defused, Maia was able to enjoy a peaceful meal and some time reading before bed. She fell asleep thinking about horses and all the things they could do for the village, wondering if she would ever see one.

Chapter 2 – Preparations

Maia walked with her father, pulling a rope tied to one side of his trader's cart. Her father pulled a rope on the other side, as they made their way across the village.

A teenage boy approached as they walked towards a small building beside a house on the far side of the central sqaure. He stood a head taller than Maia, and his skin carried the light tan of dry eucalyptus leaves.

"Hi Frank, Maia," the boy said. "We've got a load ready to go out back."

"Good," Frank replied. "Maia, you help David get the boxes on the cart, I'll go inside and sort out the inventory and pricing with his father."

"OK Dad," Maia said, as David took the rope from her father and they walked to the rear of the building. "What are you sending this time?"

"We have some jerky, and some of our special chicken seasoning, two crates of each."

"That seasoning sells pretty well in town, doesn't it?" Maia asked.

"It does, and its a great way to use the scraps of the chickens. Just dehydrate it to hell, and pulverise it into a powder. Makes a good stock for broths, adds flavour to soups, people down the mountain seem to like it. And we haven't killed anybody with it yet."

"That's a dark thought..."

They arrived where the crates were stacked, and stood one on either side as they lifted them onto the small cart. Soon the crates were properly arranged, and they took up the ropes to pull it with much effort and several pauses around to the front of the building.

"Are you getting anything from town this trip?" Maia asked.

"No, Dad will just put the money aside for next time, unless the village needs it for something sooner. We really have no use for money here, it's only helpful when we need something brought back from down the mountain. Anything we need here we can barter for."

"Uncle has requested books," Maia said.

"That crazy old guy always requests books."

"He's not crazy," Maia snapped. "He just has different priorities to the rest of us."

"I guess," David replied. "The things he learns from those books do come in handy sometimes. I guess that's why the village puts up with him pottering around that big house all day not helping on the farms."

"I saw pictures of farms from the old times. Ours are nothing," Maia said. "We just have a few yards for veges and some chickens. Those old farms were enormous, the same crop as far as the eye could see, and huge machines to harvest it all."

"Yeah, I've seen one of those when I went to school at Uncles. He used to love to show the old times to us kids, didn't he?"

"He says he doesn't want us to forget."

"I think maybe we should," David said. "I mean, sure they had all those amazing things, but look what it got them in the end. Nearly wiped us all out, didn't it?"

"That's why," Maia replied. "Uncle worries if we forget, we'll make the same mistakes again. Besides, if we can preserve some of the technologies, the ideas, we might be able to do good with them."

"Like the fire breaks? And the plumbing? Yeah, you might have a point there."

They stood in silence for a while, waiting for their fathers to come outside, but they must have been tied up with some complex haggling for the trader's commission. After a while, David sat on the cart, and Maia sat opposite him.

"This village wasn't around in the old times, was it?" David asked.

"No."

"So doesn't that make it strange? Being so concerned with remembering? It's not like our home is a part of that history."

"But it is," Maia replied. "You know the name of our village, right?"

"Gospers."

"Yeah, do you know why?"

"No, I don't remember."

"This was one of the places where everything started. The end of the old times."

"Really?"

"Yes, they called it a mega blaze. Uncle claims the fires that tore this region up burned for half a year. I don't know if that's true. But it was over a hundred years ago now. This village is in the middle of what was a special protected area, a park, where the forest had to be left alone. But then it burned. The fires were enormous. They called it the Gospers Mountain megablaze in the old news reports Uncle showed me. Though the actual Gospers Mountain was a little south and west of our village. We're more in the area that was known as Wollemi."

"Wow, so the area was destroyed?"

"Yeah, two or three days walk in any direction, and you wouldn't leave the fire ground. Even so, the rulers of the time were too blind, or stupid, to act on the changes which made it so bad."

"So that's why he wants us to remember?"

"Yes, Uncle says that we have to preserve the history of this place, and the end of the old times starts as part of that history."

They fell silent again, until Maia turned to face him, suddenly enthused.

"You know, there used to be loads of towns and cities down the mountain?"

"Yeah, I've heard that. Most of them are gone now."

"They are, but I'd love to see them anyway. I'd like to explore whatever's left, maybe find some books for Uncle's library."

"Is there much left of them?"

"Maybe not the towns, a bunch of them were levelled completely. In the final days of the old times, when they'd burned in the fire seasons or washed away in the wet times, and they still had some of the old machinery, they came in and destroyed the ruins of a lot of the old towns. The people were gone, so I guess they figured they'd let nature take back the land. I think people felt guilty for destroying so much forest, and they needed more forest to try to stop the end from coming. That's what Uncle says."

"It's ancient history anyway," David said. "None of that stuff really matters now. What matters is the village, and making sure we look after this place. We have to keep the forest alive and still keep enough food for everybody. That's the balance we have to keep. That's why we do so much preparation for the fire season."

"I won't argue with that," Maia said. "But I'd still love to see those places. The towns were incredible – so many people in one place, all living and working together. Bigger than the towns we trade with now. Uncle says the city is still there, the big one, but it's pretty much empty of people."

"Then shouldn't you go there? If the place is as big as they say, and the people are gone, couldn't you find a heap of stuff left behind?"

"Maybe, but Uncle says it's too dangerous there."

"Why?"

"Well, he says the few people who are there are territorial, but more so, if you think about it, the biggest city near us was called Sydney. It had more than three million people in it."

"Three million? Wow."

"Yeah, and now it has a few tribes, scattered around, controlling small areas, with the rest of the city abandoned. Uncle says there are less than fifty thousand left, but that they are aggressive to strangers because food is scarce in the city."

"Why?"

"In the middle of the city, they trade for food from outsiders. Apparently there are big markets where people take produce for sale, and the city people trade in artefacts they salvage, or building materials, that sort of thing. But in the city itself, it's harder to grow food for yourself, at least that's what Uncle says."

"I'd rather live here. It's peaceful," David said. "And

we can grow what we need, all we have to do is protect our area in the fire season."

"It is peaceful," Maia said. "But I still want to see those other places. I think I'll always come home though."

"You going to go with your father? For the trading trip this time?"

"I hope he'll let me. I went once last year, it was a good trip. Tiring though. We walked while the dogs pulled the cart, and it was slow going."

"But you didn't go far, did you?"

"Only to a town down the mountain called Windsor. It seemed like a long way, but compared to how people travelled in the old times, it's no distance at all. Windsor still has a huge amount of the old buildings. A lot of them are abandoned now, but that means you can find somewhere to camp under a roof easily, I wonder if they mind travellers squatting in the empty houses?"

"I think I can guess why you liked it then," David said. "All those old buildings to explore, look for stuff."

"Yeah, that's right. I even found a book for Uncle. The Windsor people ask you not to take things because they claim ownership of all artefacts in the buildings, but dad let me sneak that one thing out. He said the town would have asked me to pay for it, but I don't have my own money yet."

Frank came out then, and waved for them to follow.

"David, help us out for a bit will you?"

"Yes, Sir."

David and Maia pulled the cart again, following as Frank rushed down the road. They passed a small home, waving to the elderly lady tending the gardens. Her home was a small square shed on wheels. Like much of the village, it was an artefact of the old times converted to a domicile.

Five years ago, Maia remembered, they had moved that house when the fires last threatened the main village. She hoped that wouldn't happen again soon, but knew they were overdue for a bad season.

"Hurry up, you two," Frank hollered as he strode through a rickety gate some distance ahead.

With a lot of effort as the path wound up an incline, the pair struggled and strained, until finally they reached the gate and turned, carefully hauling the cart through and up the walkway to a house constructed against the side of another old times artefact. Uncle once said it was called a bus.

They continued around the end of the home and out the back, where a large herb garden was being tended by a family, two grown ups and three small children. Frank was already speaking to the father as they dropped the ropes and waited.

"You two, grab that crate of dried herbs by the back door and load it up." Frank yelled.

"Yes Sir," David called, while Maia smiled and nodded.

The crate was heavy, but not as heavy as the last ones. Together they carried it to the cart and loaded them up. Maia took a rope from a small box on the front of the cart, and began work securing the load.

"Just a moment, kid," Frank called out. "I'll run next door and grab one more. Wait there."

Maia waited as her father dissapeared for several minutes, returning shortly carrying a crate on his own.

"Show off," Maia teased.

Frank ignored her and hoisted the crate on top of the pile on the cart, beside the one with the herbs, so they were stacked three high. Taking the rope, he bagan to tie it off, tossing the loose end over the cart to the other side. The cart was on slightly uneven ground, and the crates wobbled as he worked. The two on top slid slightly.

"Dad," Maia said, intending to warn him, but it was too late.

As Frank pulled the rope from the downhill side, the crates toppled, then the cart tipped over, and the entire load tumbled down on top of him.

"Dad!" Maia screamed, rushing in to help.

With David's help, and the family from the herb farm rushing to help as well, they quickly moved all the crates, and found Frank's foot caught under the tipped cart. It was twisted in a painful looking fashion, and blood was beginning to soak his sock.

"Damn it," Frank seethed, clutching at his leg as he winced. "I think it's broken."

"It sure is," the father of the family said. "Looks like a nasty one. You won't be going on that trip."

Frank had a troubled expression as he looked at his daughter, his thoughts playing across his face, his concern plain to everyone.

"Maia," Frank said. "Do you think you're ready go down the mountain on your own?"

Chapter 3 – Leaving Home

Maia and Frank went over the details of the trade goods several times, and Frank made sure she had everything in writing as well, along with all the villagers' requests for goods to come back if available.

"Don't forget," Frank said. "Don't take any risks. It's been ten years since I last encountered strangers in the mountains, but there's always a first time. There are still wandering desperate people out there, just like every time in human history. If you get in trouble, save yourself, then the dogs if you can, but leave the cart."

"I'll be fine, Dad," Maia said.

"Remember, the harnesses have the guide rope threaded through them, the couplings are greased, it will slide through easily and the dogs will get away from danger if you cut it at the pommel on the cart."

"I know dad. But we've never had to do that. Don't worry."

"And when you get to Windsor, don't let them try any silly games like stinging you for rent on the empty houses. You know their rules, so play by those rules, and don't get taken for a ride."

"I know dad," Maia said. "I'll take the dogs up to Uncle's, and see what he needs before I go."

"Your mother doesn't want you to go."

"I know, Dad."

David came along then, jogging up to the house where Maia and Frank were talking on the verandah. He paused for a moment, hands on knees, his dark hair falling over his face.

"Wait, " David said. "I'll come with you, I mean, if you want. It's a long way to go alone."

"That's kind of you, David," Maia said. "But don't you have things to do here?"

"Well, yeah, but..."

"David," Frank said. "I appreciate you offering to protect my daughter, but we need you here right now. With me off my feet, and with the fire season approaching fast, you'll be needed around the village to help with the breaks, and to fight back any fire which comes close. In fact, I was talking to your father, and he was going to need your help today to check all the channels from the reservoir, to make sure we can get the water where we need it if something were to happen."

"Yes Sir," David said. "Well, be careful then, Maia. Please come home safe."

"I will," she said. "What's gotten into you?"

"I just..."

"Hey, can you help me get the dogs hooked up?" Maia asked.

"Sure," David replied, brightening.

Together, they walked around the house to the small lean to where the cart was stored, Artemis following. Maia pulled a bundle of harnesses and ropes from a shelf and opened a gate into the yard behind the house.

"Nix, Es, Jess, 'ko," she called, four of the large white dogs answering her summons and trotting out.

Nix was boisterous and excited as usual, the others a bit calmer. She tossed the bundle to the ground and fished out a harness, grabbing the nearest dog and wrestling him into it. Nix whined as she worked, his exuberance making it difficult. David picked up a harness, and tried to copy what she had done with Es.

By the time David was finished, Maia had expertly done the other two. She walked to the gate where the rest of the dogs waited, not breaking the boundary they had been trained to respect. The harnessed dogs sat where they were, waiting for their human to finish and give them instructions. All except Nix, who circled and whined impatiently.

"Raph, Rosie, Saturn, Mini," Maia called, and four more dogs ran out to greet her, before she closed the gate.

Several more dogs watched from behind the fence. Maia reached over and patted each upturned face before turning away.

"Don't worry you guys, we'll be back soon enough."

They harnessed the four dogs she had brought out, then Maia took the guiding line and threaded it through all the harnesses in order, while being careful to correctly thread it through the pulling ropes which slotted into each harness.

"That's a complicated setup," David said.

"It's so the dogs don't get hurt. They pull with the muscles in their shoulders and chest, not their backs. But even so, we have to be careful. They weren't bred for this work, so I'll be taking it slow with a lot of breaks. They can do it, but they wouldn't cope with too much in a session."

"I was wondering, why does the pup have a longer name?" David asked as she worked.

"Artemis? She doesn't. They all have longer names. But when you have to call them, a shortened version is easier for them to pick out of a command so they know who has to do something. Nix is Phoenix. Es is Esmeralda. They know their full names as well, but will always respond to the short one, and it's quicker to say in an emergency."

"So Artemis will be what? Art?"

"Probably. When she learns it. We don't abbreviate too much when they're young. Anyway, there we go, all hooked up. I'm going to take them up to Uncle's, and see if he needs anything before I leave."

"OK then," David said, shuffling awkwardly. "I should get back to my dad, he'll be wanting to get up to the reservoir soon, before the day gets too warm. Have a great trip."

"Alright," Maia said, resting a hand on his shoulder. "Thanks for your help, and your concern. You're a good friend."

She walked to the leading edge of the cart and tapped the crates with a knuckle as David watched.

"Hike!" she commanded, and the dogs began pulling.

The wheels creaked as the cart lurched out of the ruts in the ground, where years of use had left the cart's mark under the lean to. As they passed around the house, David watched, until the first dog rounded the house and he sighed, turning to walk home.

Maia smiled to herself, thinking perhaps he wasn't all bad. But something urged her not to entertain him. She had a feeling something more suitable was waiting in her future than to just be David's girl. Her mother called her stubborn, but Maia felt she had to be true to herself, and would remain so as long as it took.

"Left," Maia commanded as they passed onto the road outside the house, heading through the village.

She waved at the neighbours as she passed them. Old Beryl, who had buried her husband the previous summer, then the Newtons, who were tending their herbs, and on to the far end where the lane to uncle's passed into the trees.

The cart jostled and groaned over the rough gravel roads, and Maia remembered the tar and concrete of Windsor, wishing for a moment they could have better roads here. But the village was established after the end of the old times, when the government had faltered and the services needed for such projects were gone.

So her ancestors built this place for themselves, not wanting to be a part of the lawlessness down the mountain. Her father's father's father had been among the first children of the village, and it survived that long without the greed of the old times returning to ruin their little paradise.

She smiled to herself, thinking she would miss the village whenever she travelled, but she would travel none the less. The knowledge she gained from Uncle and his teachings left her wanting to see the world for herself, even as she grew to love her home all the more for the peacefulness she felt here.

The cart rumbled to the front step of Uncle's house. It was simple by the later standards of the old times, she knew, but she looked up at the building, comparing it not for the first time with the more humble dwellings of the village.

"I wonder what will happen to this place when Uncle's gone?" she pondered. "He has no children. I hope the village doesn't destroy his library. This place is the only place in the village for learning or preserving history. It would be a shame if that was lost."

Maia left the cart, gave a hand signal for the dogs to stay, and entered the house. She made her way to the study, where she found uncle reading a book, a cup of tea sitting cold on the table beside him.

"Uncle," she said. "Im taking the cart to Windsor. I wanted to see if you needed anything."

He smiled, and stood. Walking to her.

"Child, I only need you to come home safe. Aside from that, you know exactly the things I would want for this place. I'm getting old and I have everything I need."

"So the usual then," Maia replied. "Any books I can find, or working devices, if the price is right."

"And don't forget, if you can find any horses, do that for you. Don't squander the opportunity on the needs of other people. Finding horses is something you want, so get out there and find some. If not this trip, one day. Seeking the things you desire is a good thing for your soul. If you do everything only for others, you'll regret it later."

"I will, and even if it's not just for me, I'll find your horses too," Maia said enigmatically.

"What do you mean?" Uncle said.

"The books, the devices, those are your horses. I desire the horses, you desire the books. We both desire knowledge and history. So I'll find your horses, as well as my own."

"Thank you, Child," Uncle said with a smile.

Suddenly, he began coughing, and stumbled, reaching for support and missing the wall. Maia rushed to grab him, holding his arm with concern as she looked at his face.

"Uncle, what's wrong?"

"Nothing to worry about. It's just a bit of a cold I think. I shouldn't be wandering in the forest at night so much. I was out late the other night looking for owls."

"Owls? Why?"

"I thought I could hear one calling recently. I haven't seen an owl since I was a child. I never found any signs of it though. But even this time of year, the chill can get to you in the mountains."

"Then that's another one of your horses," Maia said as she led him back to his chair. "I'll find an owl for you, I promise, my dear Uncle."

"Thank you child. But you must be going. You need to get a good start on your journey today, if you want to get to Windsor on time."

"Yes, Uncle. Shall I fetch you a blanket before I go? Or some fresh tea?"

"The blanket would be good. Don't bother with tea, I didn't drink the last one, I guess I'm just not in the mood for it right now. I'll fetch some hot soup myself in a little while."

Once he was settled in the chair, Maia walked to a cupboard and fetched a blanket. She wrapped it over him carefully, deep concern showing on her face for her mentor.

"Please don't go making yourself ill while I'm gone," she said, taking his hand in her own. "I'll be back before you know it."

"Thank you, Child," he said, smiling at her. "Enjoy the journey. I hope you find some treasures."

"Good bye, Uncle," she said, walking from the room and back out to the dogs.

Artemis greeted her enthusiastically as she reached them. Maia picked the pup up and placed her on the front of the cart, signalling for her to sit and stay as she quickly checked the harnesses hadn't been tangled by movement of the dogs while she was inside.

Satisfied, she clapped and the dogs began the long walk back through the village. She waved again as she passed each of her neighbours, before setting out beyond the lower boundary of the village onto the rugged trail which led down the mountains.

Chapter 4 – First Day

The cart wobbled and jostled as Maia and the dogs made their way through the trees. Every now and then, they passed a fire break, the ones near the village being better cleared than the later ones, some of which hadn't been tended to in a while.

After about an hour, she reached an area where blackened trees hinted at a small fire which had passed through the area in the last season. She recalled her father and the other villagers leaving the village to tend to breaks in the area and ensure the fire didn't spread.

She continued walking, following the familiar trail. Soon, she reached a sheer cliff, which dropped away from her feet, a late fog dusting the trees in the canyon far bellow. She turned the cart east to continue a while along the edge, following the canyon as it meandered towards the coast.

It was slow going. In this area, the trail was not well maintained, and the rocky ground was subject to the vagaries of the bush. Maia looked over the edge, straining to see the creek at the bottom.

"It's Coolongooba creek," she muttered, remembering from an old map at Uncle's house.

She would follow the cliff edge until she reached a point she could descend to the creek below, and planned to stop there for a longer break. The dogs could rest and drink, and she would continue in the afternoon.

Maia pulled out the papers her father had given her, detailing the inventory and what the villagers required. The back sheet was a small hand drawn map, and she looked at it carefully.

Once she was at the creek, she would make her way down the creek until it reached the Capetree River, near the western edge of the mountains. Then her journey would turn east. The Capetree River trail was well kept, as people used it to travel to the villages on that side of the mountain.

There had been several settlements like Gospers established after the end of the old times, because the survivors didn't want to stay in the empty towns, facing whatever dangers remained there. They thought the few towns that weren't destroyed might still hold disease or something worse.

She would follow Capetree River for a day, then cross overland to the south, and follow the Colo River for another two days, before cutting across country via what she hoped was still a clear road to an area known as Richmond.

It was not going to be easy. But she had done it before, with her father. She remembered Richmond. It had the look of an enormous town, to her eyes. But it was barren ground now. Richmond was one of the towns destroyed in the end of the old times.

Maia recalled thinking how big the town must have been, and her father telling her it was small, compared to the city, which still stands on the coast, an abandoned tribute to excess. She would pass through Richmond, and arrive in Windsor that same day.

She reached a point where the trail opened out into a large cleared area with patches of grass among the rocks.

"Halt!" Maia called, dragging a flagon of water from the cart, and a bowl.

One at a time, she gave water to the dogs, before releasing the guide rope and allowing them off for a break. She then lifted Artemis down and gave her water, before allowing her to wander off to nature's call.

She watched over the dogs carefully, calling any back who wandered too far, but they were well trained and would not run away. Climbing on the front of the cart, Maia sat and relaxed, until the dogs were all settled, laying on the ground around her. She then gave each dog another chance at a drink, before putting the flagon and the bowl away.

She pulled a small pack from near where she was sitting and opened it, taking out a piece of jerky and chewing it. She took out two more pieces, and broke them up, tossing a treat to each of the dogs, before giving a piece of her own to Artemis, who lay beside her on the cart, chin on Maia's leg as she chewed the jerky.

Leaning back against the crates, Maia closed her eyes, enjoying the warm sun on her face as it washed away her fatigue, replacing it instead with a contented lethargy she knew she should not give in to.

Reluctantly, Maia climbed off the cart and picked up the guide rope.

"OK, In place!" she called.

The dogs, seemingly as reluctant as Maia, nevertheless grouped up and allowed her to reconnect them to the cart as Artemis ran between them, her puppy exuberance insulting given she had ridden on the cart the whole day.

Once she was done, Maia signalled the dogs to pull, and they continued on their way. The way was smoother now, and soon she reached a point where a smooth trail led down into the gully. A large pebbled beach stretched along the creek's edge.

It was sooner than she remembered, but Maia chose to go down anyway. She had only made the journey a couple of times and was clearly remembering wrong the time it took. Or perhaps her father had gone slower because of her.

As she descended, Maia thought she heard noises in the trees, but put it down to nerves on her part. She continued, enjoying the scenery and the stillness. The water in the creek moved slowly, with occasional trickling sounds from places where it ran over rocks.

Reaching the bottom, she called the dogs to a halt, thinking she would stop again here, and let them swim. As she reached the guide rope, Maia heard many heavy footsteps on the gravel, turning to see a group of eight men running towards her. They looked none too friendly, and were brandishing weapons.

"Shit," Maia muttered, the uncharacteristic swear coming unbidden as a rain of rocks peppered the ground around her feet.

Turning back to the cart, she quickly undid the guide

rope and shouted at the dogs.

"Run! Go home! Free dogs! Go home!" she shouted as she darted between them, ensuring the ropes fell away as the dogs bolted. Then she turned to the cart and scooped Artemis into her arms. Turning to run, Maia felt the sudden impact as a rock slammed into her head.

She stumbled, dropping Artemis, then fell as she saw stars with the impact of a second stone. Maia fell to her knees, and looked up in time to see Es and Nix disappear into the trees, the others already gone.

Artemis stayed by her mistress, guarding her as the group of men arrived at the cart. The pup barked and growled as a burly man strode up to the girl, ignoring the pup as she bit down on his arm. The man roughly grabbed Maia's hair and hauled her to her feet.

"Well now, look what we have here," the man growled. "She's a pretty little thing. I think I'll enjoy me a piece of her tonight."

"Barry, No!" another man shouted. "She's a Wollemi girl. The people in those mountain villages believe in purity and all that rubbish. She'll be a virgin. She'll fetch a high price if she stays that way."

"But Boss, look at her!" Barry whined. "She's a lovely bit and all..."

"And she's going to stay a lovely bit, unless you can pay the going rate for a slave girl who looks like that and is still untouched. Can you pay it?"

"No, Boss."

"Hey Boss," said another man.

"What is it, Carl?" the one called boss asked.

"What's a Wollemi girl?"

"Are you daft?" Boss snapped. "This here entire region used to be the Wollemi National Park, back when such a thing existed. She's from here, so she's a Wollemi girl. Get it?"

"No Boss. But I'll believe it anyway."

"You do that, Carl," Boss said. "You're thick as three planks, Carl. Go and get the car. Take Barry, I don't want him handling the merchandise."

Barry dropped Maia, and she hit the ground hard.

Artemis rushed to her lap, licking her face before turning to guard her from the remaining men. Boss approached her slowly.

"Now then Missy," boss growled. "You're going to call that mutt off, and then you won't get hurt, you see?"

Maia spat at him.

"Oh, you got spunk, girly."

Slowly, Maia got to her feet, scanning for a way out. Too late. The other men had her surrounded. Boss slapped her face, hard. Maia's knees hit the gravel again.

"You gotta stop thinking you have any power here, girly," Boss said. "We're taking your merchandise, we're taking you, and we're taking that pup. She should fetch some good money as well. Looks like a right good well bred dog that one. Shame to lose those others, but can't win 'em all, can we?"

"You'll pay for this," Maia snarled.

"Well, somebody will," Boss snapped. "And a right pretty penny they'll pay too. You'll be a good little slave for some city war lord, you will. And the mutt will likely go to a merchant to guard their caravans I'd expect. Johno, Luke, tie that little vixen up."

Two of the men jumped on her, and though she struggled, Maia couldn't fight them off. Before she knew it, she was tied up and tossed to the ground.

"Where we taking her, boss?" one of the men asked, "We still going to Windsor?"

"No, Windsor is off." Boss said.

"Why, Boss?" another man asked.

"Because clearly she was travelling to trade. You know where the villages in Wollemi trade?"

"Windsor?"

"Yeah, Windsor. And this little vixen clearly knows the way, so she's been there before. If we try to sell her in Windsor, you know what they'll do to us?"

"No, Boss."

"Tell you what, you go ahead and try, and I'll see you when you get back. Oh wait, no I won't. Because you'll be dead."

"Dead, boss?"

"Yeah, dead. The Windsor people like their trading partners. They like them a lot. Try to sell one of their trading partners in Windsor and you won't make it out alive."

Barry and Carl appeared at the end of the beach, dragging a large steel thing. Maia squinted, trying to get a better look. As they turned side on to drag it around a large pool of water, Maia suddenly recognised it from Uncle's pictures. It was an old car. A big one, the picture had called it an SUV.

Even for SUVs this looked big, and a sorry excuse for the machine it once was. The front section had been hollowed out, the engine and a lot of the other stuff pulled out, leaving just a frame. Inside the frame, Barry and Carl walked, pushing the car along with a lot of straining.

As they arrived, Maia could see the thing was riding much higher than in Uncle's pictures. They had emptied the thing of seats, and it was now just a shell with a few boxes inside.

Boss stepped up and opened a door, while his comrades began taking Maia's crates from the cart and moving them into the car. Once the cart was empty,

Carl strode over and scooped Maia up like a sack of grain. He carried her, as she wriggled and tried to escape, and tossed her into the car. She landed hard and winded, but turned over, only to be hit by Artemis, who was tossed in after her, a snarling, growling mess of fur and claws.

"What'll we do with her cart?" Barry asked.

"Leave it there," Boss said. "We've got no use for the thing, and it will just be added weight. It's worthless in the city. Now get moving. We have a long way to go. Hopefully we can snare a couple more traders on the way. I told you it was worth coming north. Nobody else ever farms the roads up here!"

Chapter 5 – Stolen

Frank was sitting on the verandah with his feet up, sipping a rare drink of whisky when he heard them. It was only a few days since Maia had left, and he was already concerned. But to hear the dogs coming home unattended raised a terror in him like nothing had before.

"Helen!" Frank shouted. "Helen! The dogs are back! Quickly, get help, we have to go searching for Maia!"

Helen ran from the house, passing Frank as she rushed out into the yard, where Es and Nix had just arrived, yipping, and barking as they bounced around her. The dogs were dirty, having clearly made their way across wild country without Maia's guidance.

'Ko and Jess arrived almost immediately behind them, followed by Saturn, Rosie, and Raph. Mini lagged some way behind, holding his front left paw up as he ambled along. Even from a distance, Helen could see the dried blood on the paw.

Helen ran to Mini, scooping the thirty kilogram animal up like a bag of flour, and rushing back to the house.

"No sign of Arty or Maia. I'll get this little one bandaged and settled, then we round up anybody who is available. Maia must be found. You stay put, Frank. You're no use to a search party with that broken leg."

"David!" Frank shouted at the top of his lungs, hoping the lad wasn't too far away.

"David! Gather up anybody available and get over here!"

The dogs crowded onto the verandah, curious about Frank, and why he wasn't standing up to greet them. Nix sniffed at the bandaged leg and nudged it.

"Dammit! Nix, leave it alone!"

The dogs seemed to understand then, but were clearly anxious.

"You want us to go save your mistress, don't you?"

Frank said, scratching Es on the head. "Don't worry, we'll find her, whatever has happened."

"You won't be finding anybody, Frank."

He looked up at the deep voice to see David and his father coming through the gate, three other men in tow. David went and opened the gate to the yard, ushering the dogs in. Nix refused, sitting beside Frank protectively, his whining unceasing.

"So Frank, I take it Maia didn't come back then?" David's father asked.

"No Greg," Frank replied. "The dogs have come home on their own, with no cart, no Maia, and no Arty."

"No Arty? That's her pup? At least she has one of them with her, for whatever help the puppy will be," Greg said.

"Yeah, She'll take comfort in the pup at least. She loves that little girl. I just hope she's safe."

"Even if she isn't, we'll find her and bring her home. Mark my words," Greg said.

"I know you will," Frank replied. "And whatever happened, we have to tell Windsor. They'll be expecting our usual trade, and will have to arrange something if they aren't getting it."

*   *   *

David and Greg, along with four others from the village, trailed the cart to the clearing on the clifftop.

"You can see by the tracks Maia stopped here for a rest," Greg said. "But she wasn't abducted here, and the dogs continued pulling the cart when she left."

"We should keep moving then," David said. "If she's laying somewhere hurt, we have to get to her fast."

"That's true," Greg said, "But we shouldn't jump to any conclusions yet. Let's get moving."

The group continued on, following the tracks of the cart, wherever Maia had crossed dirt, picking the trail a piece at a time over the rocky ground.

David walked close to the edge, looking down from time to time in case the cart had gone over the side. He couldn't see much, but sometimes the creek at the bottom came into view through the trees.

He cast his gaze forward, tracing the creek through the canyon, and saw a section up ahead where a long pebbly beach had formed. Then he saw something there, and squinted, trying to see what it was. He stopped.

"Down there!" David shouted, pointing. "The cart is on that beach!"

Picking up the pace, the men walked as fast as was safe until they found the path Maia had used to descend. They rushed down to the beach, and approached the cart with rapid caution.

"Look at all these tracks!" David exclaimed.

"Something big, some kind of vehicle," Greg said, studying the disturbed ground, "And several men."

"So it looks like she was abducted after all," David said sadly.

"We've never had a problem with thieves or highwaymen before," Greg said, "but I heard from Frank last summer that the people in Windsor reported them active in the south."

"So they're expanding their operations into our area?" one of the other men asked with a snarl, "That's not good news at all. We'll have to do something."

"But you know as well as I do, Lucas," Greg said. "We aren't equipped with the manpower or the weaponry to take out an organised gang. We should report this to Windsor. They have a militia, and a lot of men at their disposal."

"Then what are we waiting for?" David said, "We should get there as fast as possible. If they can start a wider search, it might save Maia's life."

"I doubt her life is in danger," Greg said. "But her freedom..."

"What do you mean?" Lucas asked.

"Given they took her and the merchandise, they'll probably have a desire to sell her into slavery for as much as they can get. That's how these gangs would operate. Otherwise she'd still be here, dead or alive."

"How do you know about these things?" David asked.

"I read books about crime in the old days, Uncle has a

few in that house. It's a bit of a guilty pleasure. There were some nasty criminals in those days. It's fun to try to understand how they think."

"Sometimes, I think you're a strange man, Greg," Lucas muttered.

"I suggest we hot-foot it to Windsor," Greg said, Ignoring Lucas' comment. "David, Lucas, you two take the cart back to the village and let them know what we found."

The men all muttered their agreement, and together the group set off at a jog, leaving Lucas and David to pull the cart home. The joggers still had a long way to go to reach their destination.

*   *   *

Greg strode out in front of the group as they finally reached the outer limits of the Windsor controlled area. It was a small town called Upper Colo. A handful of families lived there, and were happy to point them in the right direction, past a faded ancient sign that read "Comleroy Road."

It was a worn and weathered old road, blue metal crumbling and giving way to the local grasses, but still well travelled and so reasonably clear. A young woman from Upper Colo accompanied them, saying she had business down that road as well.

"What village did you say you came from?" the woman asked.

"Gospers," Greg replied.

"Oh, that's up in the mountains right? In the old Wollemi park?"

"Yeah..."

"Funny, there's a creek just nearby called Gospers Creek. It's a pretty common name around here."

"Really?"

"Yeah, it is. Is it Frank, the trader who comes down usually?"

"Yeah, but he's injured. He sent his daughter instead."

"I met her last year when they passed through. Seemed like a smart kid. But I haven't seen anybody recently."

"No..." Greg said, hesitant to say more.

"Has something happened? It seems unusual to have you men running to Windsor with nothing to trade."

"We..." Greg said, slowly, "Don't exactly know. We found the cart, empty, no sign of the girl..."

"So you're looking for her?"

"Well, yes, but there's a problem. We also found the tracks of a larger vehicle, and several men. We fear she was abducted."

"So those mongrels from down south have come north then..."

"It seems that way."

"You can't take them on alone."

"I know. We'll speak to the militia in Windsor. Perhaps they can help."

"They may do. They've been running a campaign against the highwaymen to the south this last year. A reasonably successful one at that."

"I wonder if that's what sparked the move north?" Greg asked.

"It might be, and that might be why they help you. They'll want to know all you can tell them, at any rate."

"How long is the walk into Windsor from here?" Greg asked. "My map from Frank doesn't really say."

"You won't make it in time to speak to the militia today. You've got about eight or nine hours walking ahead, without breaks. So it will be evening when you arrive."

"That's fine," Greg said.

"You might have gotten there quicker, had you continued as you were going and headed down Putty road, but there are some recent land slips along there, and some very badly damaged stretches of road which would make it more dangerous."

"Then this route will be fine," Greg said.

"Have you got a preferred place to stay?"

"No. I'm not sure what Frank does, but he has said there are a lot of empty buildings to use."

"If you do that, you'll likely get a visit from the Militia with a rent collector. Frank would have had an agreement set up, which he'd settle after the trade. But you have nothing to trade, so you might have trouble convincing them to let you do that."

"So what do we do then?"

The woman shrugged.

"We'll have to just play it by ear."

"If you don't light a fire or make a lot of noise, they may not find you..." she said.

"And how do we find them? Tomorrow I mean."

"Just head into the middle of town. They have signs to the court painted all over the place. You'll find it. The court is the group of buildings where they run the militia and their town government from, and it's where the market is as well, which Frank would have marked on the maps he gave you I'd guess."

"We will see then," Greg said. "I hope they will see us."

"They will see you," the woman said. "Whether they do any more, you will have to wait and see."

"I hope so."

"Well, I'll leave you here," the woman said. "I'll be spending my day here, collecting some plants for medicine. I wish you luck, men of Gospers. I hope the girl is returned to you soon."

"Farewell, then," Greg said.

As the woman left them, the men sped into a jog, and made good time down Comleroy Road. As the sun lowered to the peaks in the west, they reached the end of the worn out road, at an intersection with a sign, battered and faded. It indicated a left hand turn to Windsor, along a bigger road, in slightly better condition, called Bells Line of Road.

Re-energised by the nearness of the destination, the men increased their pace as they ran east. After an hour of this hard slog, they passed a sign which read "Nor Ri hmo d." The sun was setting behind them, a vibrant orange tinging the sky, with darkness ahead and low clouds rolling in from the coast.

"What do you make of that?" one of the men said.

"It's badly damaged," Greg said, looking carefully at a crumpled parchment. "The last hundred and fifty years have been hard on these places. But Frank's map says North Richmond. I think it's safe to guess that's where we are."

"Should we stop?"

"No, look around you, Graham."

While the ground bore heavy scarring to indicate a sizeable settlement, there was little else left to show for the town which once stood here. Rubble was everywhere. And the rubble was overrun with grasses, weeds, and occasional trees.

In spite of the vegetation, it was a desolate place. As they crossed a river over a crumbling, concrete bridge, they saw they still had a long run ahead, and it was getting darker, fast.

"We should perhaps find a place to rest, and continue in the morning," Greg said.

"How far do you suppose it is?" Graham asked.

"That woman said eight or nine hours from there. We've been going six or seven at a guess. So too far to go in the dark, in unfamiliar terrain. If we see some buildings, we'll take our chances. I'd rather not be sleeping in the open if it rains."

They ran on, and after nearly an hour, reached Richmond. Unlike it's northern companion, this place wasn't levelled completely. Several buildings remained. The town seemed uninhabited.

One of the first buildings, to the left of the road, was what seemed to the men an enormous house. Two stories, red bricks, concrete arches, and vacant. The windows long since smashed, the door long since burned away, the shell of the building was still decent, and the roof looked intact.

The men cautiously entered, and made their way to a room which must have once been the kitchen. They set up camp, just as the rain started to patter on the roof.

Chapter 6 – Seeking help

Maia cursed herself for choosing to travel alone. She understood that these kinds of criminals were not normally in her region, but even so, she blamed herself. She sighed. In Maia's world, there was nothing in a person's appearance to create any notion they might be good or bad people. Only actions demonstrated evil intent, and by that time, it was too late to run.

The SUV rumbled along the rough ground as the bandits took her away from her intended destination. Maia pulled herself into a sitting position, so she could see out the window of the vehicle. Since she was sitting on the floor, she could only just see out over the edge of the glass.

Maia was lost. She knew it was her fifth day in the SUV, forced to use a bucket for the toilet and passed meagre food in each day, and not enough water. She'd happily kill the men for a drink, but didn't have the strength to do much.

The SUV had rumbled along the creek heading west, and down hill, to follow a river inland before turning south. Maia had no idea exactly where they were now, and they were far from anything she might recognise. She was left alone for the most part, except when Boss would reach an arm in to steady the steering wheel or turn it on some of the rougher places. He had explained they removed the original, complicated steering and did something but she hadn't listened to his boastful description. She wasn't about to be supportive of his efforts.

Maia was staring at the passing barren landscape, the forest in the distance casting a blue haze over the mountains. A sudden pounding noise snapped her out of her thoughts as Boss thumped the outside of the window, in front of her face.

"Get down you little bitch!" he shouted. "We're

coming into Blackman's Flat, and we'll be going on to Lithgow from there. You're not to be seen at all in either town. Do I make myself clear?"

She nodded, and lay down in the back of the SUV. The town names were only that to her. She had read of the places but had no real knowledge of them.

"Where are you taking me?" she asked, not expecting an answer.

Boss scowled at her through the glass for a moment, then glanced over his shoulder before leaning closer.

"We're going to go back through the mountains via Blackheath," he said in a soft snarl, "And down into the city. We'll find a buyer there at the market."

"You really think I won't escape along the way?"

"You won't escape. It's a gamble, taking that route, but worthwhile. We know it well, and you don't."

"I can run fast," Maia said.

"Not fast enough," Boss replied. "Behave yourself, and we might be inclined to ensure a good buyer."

"You won't be getting any buyer if I have my way."

"You've still got spirit. That'll raise the price. But mind it doesn't raise my fist, girl."

"You wouldn't damage your merchandise," Maia said.

"Do you want to risk that?" Boss replied. "We had no intention of finding a girl to sell on this trip, we'll cover our costs with the other goods you brought us. If the profit on you drops, it's still all profit."

"I could scream in the towns..."

"Here on out, you won't find help. They help themselves, you're a stranger in these parts. It would benefit you to remember that."

"In that case, why is it so important I stay out of sight?"

"The militia from Windsor might be hanging around the roads west of the city, and they wouldn't take kindly to us selling girls, so you keep that pretty head down. Or else it won't be pretty anymore."

"So the towns people might tell the militia? Good to know."

"Stop thinking, you smart arse little whore. Sit in there, keep your head down, and shut up. If I hear another word, I might talk to you with something other than my words. Or I might let Barry in there. His birthday's coming up."

*   *   *

Greg and the men woke late, the morning sun already blasting the wet ground. They packed their things and left the house, hoping to make a short dash into Windsor. As they walked out onto the road, a lean man was walking towards them, coming from Windsor.

"Hello!" the man shouted, waving an arm over his head as he jogged to meet them. "Heading for Windsor?"

"Yes. We have an urgent matter to speak to the militia about."

"I haven't seen your faces before. Where are you from?"

"Gospers," Greg said, seeing no reason to lie to this stranger.

"I thought you must be from the mountains," the man said. "I'm Jared. I live up in Colo Heights. You probably came through there then."

"Yes, we did."

"You've never been down to Windsor before, have you?" Jared asked.

"No..."

"Yeah, I can tell, if you had, you would have stopped somewhere else, or pushed on to Windsor in the night."

"Why?" Greg asked.

"Because if they hear you stayed in a house in Richmond for the night, nobody in that town will speak to you. They won't want you anywhere near them. You can expect a rough welcome from the Militia too. They have to make a show of protecting the people."

"Protecting the people?" Greg said. "From what?"

"Disease," Jared said. "Why do you think North Richmond was flattened?"

"Oh," Greg said.

"Yeah, it was a hundred years ago, and then a bit, the year twenty-sixty-three, but it was after the world went to

36

hell. The remaining government of the time sent the machines out from the city and they levelled the place deliberately. But all the residents were already dead or dying by then."

"And Windsor was spared?"

"Not completely, but enough that the town survived. And they stopped anybody from Richmond getting in. You have to understand, those viruses that were killing people, if they got into your community, they'd wipe you out in a matter of weeks."

"Scary stuff."

"Yeah, it was. And I know the virus can't still live here, but the people in towns nearby to these places, they're terribly superstitious. Down in the city, where people were packed in, they died in the millions."

Jared turned, squinting into the morning sun, his face thoughtful as he kicked at the wet grass. He looked back at Greg.

"A few still live there, in the city, but they don't trust strangers, and they still have sickness, though a lot of it is because of how they live I think, not because of the old diseases. At any rate, If anybody asks, you stopped in Colo Heights, and came down the last leg this morning."

"Thanks, I'll remember that."

"Best that you do," Jared said. "You'll see a large cleared area ahead. It was a sports field in the old times. Right after that is an ancient railway station. Follow the rails, that's your quickest route to Windsor. Good luck, fellas."

Jared walked away, heading back the way Greg and his men had come from the day before. Greg set out towards Windsor, thankful for the chance encounter. It may have saved them a lot of trouble.

True to Jared's words, on their left after a while they found the old sports grounds. The cleared area was covered in weeds, tall grasses, and spiky shrubs now, where it wasn't pocked hard bare earth. The stands at one end, which came into view as they walked around an old ruin with signs proclaiming "Richmond School of Arts," were tumbling down, a deadly hazard to anybody foolhardy enough to enter.

The men pushed through the dry scrub, occasionally slipping in the mud left by the previous night's rain. Reaching the far side, they crossed the crumbling road to find the beginning of the railway Jared had spoken of. Rusted, buckled lines ran off into the distance.

The ballast was in poor condition, long since either washed away or stolen from many points, and the majority of the sleepers were missing. The few sleepers still there were concrete, and clearly a useful building commodity if you could be bothered to retrieve them.

The ground along side the rails was far safer, and Greg set out, the men following, careful to watch their footing. They walked for nearly two hours, until they passed Windsor Station, and saw a crudely painted sign pointing left, indicating "Windsor Courts."

They walked in that direction, along a wide road, and soon saw a worn old sign on a corner reading "Macquarie St." The signs indicated they were crossing Brabyn Street.

A short time later, they reached an enormous intersection, and across the way from them they could see where the railway sleepers had gone. They had been used to build a high wall around a large section of the town, and painted on the wall was "Windsor Courts." A tall metal gate blocked a gap in the wall on Macquarie Street.

They crossed the intersection and stood before the gate. Greg looked both ways along the structure, and could see the wall extended a full block in either direction, before turning at the next intersections. The walls enclosed a large area in a fortress against the outside world.

"State your business, strangers!" a man shouted from a short distance beyond the gate, walking towards them.

"We seek the militia, on a matter of grave urgency regarding recent occurrences in the mountains." Greg shouted back.

"What region do you hail from?" the man said as he arrived at the gate.

"We are from the village known as Gospers."

""Oh, I see," the man said. "Your trader is late. Is this urgent matter related to that?"

"It is," Greg said. "Our usual trader was injured, so his child travelled instead. She did not make it here before being set upon by unknown assailants. The goods from our village, and the girl, were taken to an unknown destination."

"I see," the guard said as he opened the gates. "This is a grave circumstance indeed. There have been many skirmishes between the militia and groups of bandits in the south of late. This may be a related incident. The militia will want to hear your full report. Enter. You will find them in the old police station to your right against the far wall of the courts."

"Thank you," Greg replied, as he led the men through.

They soon located the old police station, two armed men guarding the entry. The guards allowed them in, but Greg felt they might be more interested in stopping them leaving should anything go wrong. A large reception area confronted them, a woman of dour countenance guarding the desk.

"What do you need?" she demanded.

"We travel from the village of Gospers, with news of abduction and theft of our trade goods, and a request for assistance."

"Very well, wait here," she said, leaving through a doorway to the rear of the building.

Shortly, a firm older man, grey beard and bald head lending a fatherly but stern atmosphere to his presence came out and stood before Greg.

"What is it you want?" he demanded.

"Our trader was injured, so his daughter came in his stead. She never arrived. We located her cart a short way down the mountain, all our goods taken, and no sign of the girl. There were tracks of several men, and a large vehicle at the site of the abduction. We seek any assistance that may be possible to rescue the girl."

"And the goods?"

"They are of little concern. It is the safety of the trader's child we are most worried about."

"Very well. Our troops have long needed to expand north and west in their patrols. One of you will accompany a troop to identify the girl should they find the band of men responsible."

"I will accompany them," Greg said. "I have made a promise to her father that I would not stop until she was found."

"Very well. Your men may return home when they are ready. In the mean time, they may attend the markets and conduct any other business they may require while in the courts. You may stay in any vacant house outside the walls at no charge for tonight, given the circumstances. But should they choose to stay longer, or stay inside the court walls, payment will be required. You however, will stay in the barracks until the troop is deployed. You will be provided for, as a consulting guest of the militia."

"When will the search begin?" Greg asked.

"Likely the day after tomorrow, unless there is reason for delay. I appreciate the girl's safety is your concern, but preparations must be made. There is no point losing our men to a well prepared criminal group."

"Understood," Greg said. "I look forward to working with you."

*   *   *

Uncle wandered the forest. He had walked until after midnight every night for a week, but had seen no sign of Maia, or of those who took her. He had hoped she may have escaped her captors and fled into the forest, but it was looking less and less likely he would find his student.

The air had a chill, unusually so for the time of year, and he drew his coat close around him. As the wind whipped through the trees, he coughed. It was a brief flurry at first, but then the wracking convulsions took hold, and he coughed for a long time, the hollow empty night mocking his noise with its silence. He leaned against a tree, struggling to hold himself upright as his energy rushed from him.

Then the coughs abated, and he stayed propped against the rough bark of an ash, looking around, trying to remember his bearings. He hadn't been lost in his woods for decades, but now he felt more lost than he ever had in his life.

He sat hard, the cold ground welcoming his buttocks with a wicked sting. His breathing heavy, Uncle looked around again, feeling his age, and beginning to fret. He worried, for the first time since she had gone missing, not for Maia, but for himself.

"Perhaps I've finally over done it," he mumbled, and then he heard the sound.

"Ooo Ooo Ooo"

"Is that?" he said, suddenly excited, and scrambling to his feet..

"Ooo Ooo Ooo"

Uncle turned about, trying to pick the direction. And then as it called a third time, he was sure. He rushed through the scrub, pushing past branches of trees and driving himself headlong into the undergrowth.

Suddenly, he burst into a clearing, where an ancient tree had fallen, and there, perched on a high branch, which reached to the sky from the fallen behemoth, sat a large grey creature, staring down at him with an air of great disdain.

"Ooo Ooo Ooo" it said.

"A Tawny Frog Mouth," Uncle whispered. "Where have you been hiding all these years?"

"Ooo!" it said, with a sense of finality in its call, and then spread its mighty wings and launched itself into the night, disappearing over the trees.

"Well I'll be damned," Uncle said, smiling. "I know it's technically not an owl, but I'll take it. I'll find my horses, Maia. I hope you're out there somewhere, finding yours."

Chapter 7 – Into The City

The climb back into the mountains was long and slow. It took all eight men pushing in some places, and they had to take regular breaks. When the road ran down a slope, Boss climbed in up the front, where the steering wheel was, and worked the breaks.

Once they almost lost control as he wasn't inside the SUV in time and it started to roll away. The two men in the engine bay pumped their legs to run as fast as they could, screaming and shouting to stop the crazy thing.

"When we get to the big down hill run on the other side of the mountains, you two get out first," Boss said then. "That run will be steeper and faster than any downhill run you've pushed this thing through before."

Lithgow had passed without Maia seeing anything of the town. So had much of the landscape as Boss was being firm in his demand she stay out of sight. Curiosity was getting the better of her. It was dark outside now, and she knew the men must be tired.

"Where are we now? If it's OK to tell me," Maia asked, not sure who could hear her.

"I suppose it's pretty dull in there," came Boss's voice in reply. "We're at Mount Victoria now. We've just passed the Mitchell Ridge Lookout, which means the town is just ahead, so keep your head down and your mouth shut for a while. It's getting rather late, so we'll be stopping here for the night. I'll figure out what we do about you in a moment."

"That's a long way in a day," Maia mused.

"Yes, but my men are up for the task. To succeed in our business, we have to move father and faster than any militia who might come looking for us. That's why we risk the mountain road so late into the night. Now quiet, or I'll have to climb in there and gag you."

Half an hour later, the SUV stopped outside a house,

and Boss climbed in. Rummaging, he took a blanket from somewhere, and threw it over Maia. Not being gentle, he rolled her in it.

"Stay still, and don't make a noise, the dog stays here," he hissed at her as he dragged her in the blanket out the door, where one of the men took her over his shoulder and carried her like a sack into a building.

Soon the blanket was pulled off her, and Maia found herself in a small room. There was a tiny barred window high in one wall, and an old time toilet, with years of dust and grime caked onto it.

"We'll be right outside the door, so don't try anything," Boss said. "Just be glad we gave you privacy for the evening. I'll have Barry bring you some food later."

Maia said nothing, but wrapped herself in the blanket, even though it wasn't cold. Somehow she felt safer cocooned in the battered old thing than without it. Barry tossed her a small piece of the jerky they had stolen from her, and she chewed on it for a long while, until she felt sleep coming.

She tossed and turned uncomfortably for the night, there on the hard cold floor of the old bathroom. When morning finally came, she felt as tired as she had the night before, and didn't complain as she was wrapped in the blanket and carried back to the SUV.

The sun was barely lighting the sky in the east as they set out, and Maia closed her eyes and let sleep take hold as the vehicle jostled along the worn old road. A bit under two hours later, she woke as the SUV stopped.

Maia was about to sit up and steal a peak outside, but then she heard Boss.

"Stay down," he hissed in a firm but quiet voice. "It's Blackheath. We stop for breakfast, and move on. We'll be here about fifteen minutes. If you show your face, I'll let Barry break it."

She did as she was told, laying there as quietly as she could, listening to the sounds of a busy community as the town of Blackheath went about it's usual morning routine. Suddenly the door opened, and Boss's hand reached in to drop a small paper package on the floor.

"Eat that," he hissed. "And don't say we don't feed you well."

She whispered a nervous thank you, and reached for the pack. It was warm! She hastily opened it, to find a fresh baked meat pie inside. She smiled. Uncle had told her of the many varieties of meat pie you could buy in the old times.

He had told her how in every town, they would taste a little different, and some people took enormous pleasure in trying them wherever they were made. Maia took a tentative bite. It was delicious, the gravy not too hot, the meat though sparse was not rancid, tough, or too fatty, and the gravy had the pleasing aroma of paprika, turmeric and garram masala, spices she was only familiar with because Uncle had shown them to her a long time ago when he had bought some from a travelling merchant in Windsor. She wondered briefly how far these exotic spices had travelled to reach the bakery.

The taste over all was exquisite. A better pie than any she had tried either on the mountain or in Windsor. Maia ate it fast, her hunger overpowering her delight at the sudden and unexpected treat of quality food.

"How is it, Girl?" Barry's voice whispered. "It's OK, Boss isn't nearby. You can tell me."

"The pie?" she whispered back. "It's by far the best pie I have ever tasted," she replied, with obvious sincerity in her voice.

"That's wonderful! I'll be sure to let the baker know! But don't tell boss I spoke to you. My brother is the baker in this town, and I think he's the best baker alive. He thinks he's not, but still loves his work. I'll tell him quietly what you said. It will make him happy."

"Your brother? He's a baker? I'm sorry, I kind of assumed you'd all be from families in your line of work. In the village, people tend to carry on the family jobs"

"Yeah, in this world, nobody is born a villain. We choose our paths, even in your village. You can find a way to do what matters to you. It's not always easy, and it certainly can cause you a lot of trouble, but whatever life throws at you, you can turn it to your own benefit."

"That's," Maia said, then hesitated. "Actually really good advice, Barry. I'm sorry, I think I misjudged you. You don't seem that smart when you talk to Boss."

"We all play our role," he said. "But what matters is who we are in ourselves. We have to honour that, and stay true to it. My brother the baker has done that better than any man I know. He deserves my respect and admiration. He's managed that far better than I ever could. The rest of our family won't ever see me, because of what I've done. My brother accepts me, and keeps on baking, because to him, his own deeds are what matters, not mine."

"I'm glad you talked to me, Barry," Maia said. "You scared me before, but I think I understand you more now."

"You were supposed to be scared. That's my job. Please, for my sake, keep up the act, as long as you're with us."

"Barry! What are you doing over there?" Boss shouted from somewhere then. "Get over here, I need your help with something."

And just like that, Maia was left alone again, to quietly wonder about who she was, and who these men were, and what she would have to do when they reached the City. It didn't take long, and the men were all back and the SUV began to move again.

As instructed, Maia kept her head down, and did not see the landscape they travelled through. The road went up and down as they travelled, the men climbing onto the SUV with Boss in the front for the down hill runs.

The vehicle picked up great speed, just under the force of gravity on those runs, but they lost time pushing it up the next rise, so time saved was also time lost. Near mid day, Maia could hear sounds of people around them, but did not dare to speak up, even if Barry no longer scared her as he used to. She knew that if Boss ordered him, he was capable still of hurting her badly.

"Katoomba," Boss hissed, as if knowing her thoughts. "It will be more down hill than up from here. We will stop late tonight on the banks of the Nepean River."

The remainder of the day passed without a stop, and the speed of the SUV was scary at times as it flew down the mountain roads. Boss steered the barrelling vehicle, applying the break far less than Maia thought wise. The rest of the men clung to the sides or sat on the frame at the front so as not to be left behind.

The sun dipped early behind the mountains, casting their shadows far out into the lands below. Maia risked a peak from time to time, and was never able to see much as they wound their way through a mixture of forest and rocks. Finally they came to a stop well into the evening, and Maia sat in the SUV, listening to splashes as the men bathed in the river.

Boss gave her jerky, and she struggled to sleep, her mind turning over the possibilities that lay ahead. So it was, before sunrise, that she was awake when Boss climbed into the SUV.

"This'll be the last day of travel, and a long one," he said. 'But we can't take any chances. The Windsor Militia won't go far into the city, but we will be crossing their usual patrol territory. So I need to be sure you will be quiet."

He checked her ropes, removing the foot of length they had given her previously between wrists, so she could no longer feed herself, and gagged her. He then fitted a blindfold, and propped her against the crates.

Wrapping a rope around her and a crate, he tied her there, before dropping blankets over her body, so it would look like nothing more than goods for trade, should any militia look into the SUV.

She sat there, scared and angry, as the SUV jostled along for a little over twelve hours. The time was slow, and her position uncomfortable. She wasn't afforded toilet breaks or food that day, and by the time they arrived at their destination. She was exhausted from her worry and her body was stiff and sore when Barry reached in, dragged her out, and tossed her effortlessly over his shoulder.

Still blindfolded, she was carried some distance through a building, sounds of people, and animals surrounding her. The smells were many, and so varied as to lend no clue to her whereabouts.

She could hear hawkers shouting their best deals, and buyers haggling, and sounds of chickens, other birds familiar, and some not so familiar, as well as the scuffle of feet and all manner of noises she could not identify.

"Welcome, Stranger, to Paddy's Market," a voice cried nearby. "I would like to show you the finest blankets money can buy, far better than those you carry now."

"Not interested," Barry snarled.

"Sir, I know you will be once you feel the softne..."

There was then the sound of a fist hitting a jaw, accompanied by great jostling of Barry's shoulder, and followed by a firm thud as the hawker was laid out cold by Barry's impatient fist.

"Well, at least I know where I am," Maia thought. "Paddy's Markets. I'm amazed the place is still operating. That's a place from the old times. So, we really are in the city. What was it called? Sydney. Uncle says it's far too dangerous a place to ever travel, even though it's population is mostly gone. Yet here I am."

Suddenly Barry dropped her onto the ground, and pulled the blind fold off. It was dark, but still her eyes squinted in what light there was after a day of blindness.

She found herself in a small pen, like that of an animal. Cage bars surrounded her on three sides, a weathered brick wall on the fourth. Tattered ancient wire mesh covered the bars. Still bound, she could not move easily, so she lay there for now, allowing her body to recover from its long abuse.

Turning her head, she could see into the next pen. A huge hoofed foot scratched at the dirt, long shaggy fur hanging over the hoof, as it struck down. Maia could see raw power in that limb, and wanted desperately to see more of whatever it was.

"Lay still, Girl," Barry hissed. "I'm hanging a sheet over your pen's front, don't move until it's done. You go to secret auction tomorrow, nobody can know you're here who isn't involved."

She lay there, for several minutes. Artemis was tossed rudely in with her, yelping as she landed.

"Done, you keep the gag on, Girl, but you can move,

as much as your ropes will allow. No noise, you got it?"

She nodded her head as she forced herself into a sitting position, looking to see Barry's face through a gap pushed open in the curtain he had hung.

"Girl," Barry said. "For what it's worth, I'm sorry. But I can't let you go. Boss would kill me. Then he'd kill you. Whoever buys you tomorrow, I wish you luck."

Maia simply glared at him, not willing or able to voice her opinion on that cowardly admission, fearing the punishment that would come. She said it all with her eyes, however, and Barry shook his head, scoffed, and left, the curtain falling to hang over the pen, so no passer by would easily see her.

She glared at that fabric for a long while, until she remembered the hoofed foot. Shuffling back against the wall, she wrigged her way upright, then hopped towards the side of her pen where it was, watching her feet and the ground as she moved, to ensure she didn't fall. Finally, the cage wire and bars were in front of her and she raised her eyes.

As she looked forward, she saw fur. She tilted her face up, and found herself staring into enormous brown eyes, and a long face, a steel bit in the mouth, flared nostrils exhaling enough air to flutter her hair as the creature sniffed her scent.

"Oh..." she murmured through the gag, the surprise showing in her widening eyes.

Maia raised her arms, the hands still bound, to rest them on the cage as she leaned closer to the animal that was to be her neighbour for the night. Artemis gazed up at her master, unusually still for the pup.

"What does this mean?" she thought, staring into those big brown eyes. "It's a horse, clearly. Far bigger than the pictures I saw, but a horse just the same. What was it Barry said? Whatever life throws at you, you can turn it to your own benefit. I wonder, how can I turn you to my benefit?"

Chapter 8 – Escape

Maia leaned on the cage wall, admiring the horse for a long time. It was more beautiful to her than she had imagined. After a short time it grew bored of the girl staring. It turned away, lapped idly at a trough, and snuffled where a pile of feed had been, only the last remnants remaining to assuage it's hunger.

Artemis growled, alerting Maia to somebody outside the horse's pen. The lock rattled and the gate was swung open, into the walkway outside. A young man, about the same age as Maia's eighteen years, entered the pen, dragging a sack.

The boy was looking down as he moved, so didn't see Maia. Artemis continued to growl and the boy looked at the dog, oblivious to its master.

"Hello little one," the boy said. "You're a cute puppy, aren't you? I wonder who's selling you? I'm Alex. I'm here to feed your big friend, sorry if I disturbed you."

"Well you disturbed me," Maia snarled, her voice muffled through the gag. "And the pup is mine. Though I have no clue how we're both getting out of here."

Alex jumped at her voice and backed away, as if more scared of a human than a growling dog. He looked at her for a long moment, his eyes settling on her bound wrists.

"Oh, sorry, I didn't realise they had started using this area for prisoners. What did you do?"

"I didn't do anything, you idiot!" Maia snapped, her words barely comprehensible through the tight fabric, then calmed herself before continuing. "I was abducted while I was travelling with the trade goods from my village. They plan to sell me tomorrow."

"Sell you?" Alex gasped, as he began taking food from the sack and placing it for the horse. "That's awful!"

"But it's true," Maia said, sobbing as she sat on the ground. "They took everything, and sold it. They want to sell me. They say some warlord from the city will pay a lot for me. All I want to do is go home."

"I'll take you home," Alex said, reaching through a gap in the wire covering the bars to untie her gag. "I mean, the city might be rough, but there are still rules here. Nobody can be sold. We don't allow slavery."

"Thanks, but do you really think the kind of people who abduct girls and steal trade goods give a damn about your city rules?"

"Fair point. Do you know when they're selling you?"

"I only know tomorrow."

"Then we don't have a lot of time. I'm supposed to be looking after the horse. So I can get in and out of here easy. Getting you out will be harder."

"So it's impossible..."

"No, just harder. But if I wait and come back a bit later, after the traders are away drinking, we'll be fine. Trust me."

Maia looked at Artemis, who had stopped growling and was watching the boy with a critical air. The dog tilted her head to the left, questioning him.

"OK," Maia said. "Artemis seems to have decided to give you a chance, so I'll trust her opinion."

"Good. Be ready to leave at a moment's notice," Alex said. "And to that end..."

He rummaged in his pockets, and pulled out a small knife. He poked it through the wires of the cage, and it dropped to the floor near Artemis.

"Use that to cut your ropes. But be careful. If your sellers come to look, you have to look like you're still tied up."

"Thanks, Alex."

"Oh, one other thing," Alex said as he folded the top of the sack and began to drag it back out of the pen. "What's your name, girl?"

"I'm Maia."

"Good to meet you, Maia. I'll be back. Trust me."

"But what if you're caught? Won't you get in trouble?"

"Don't worry. If I explain what you told me to my boss, she'll have my back one hundred percent."

As the gate closed and the lock rattled, Maia shuffled her way to the knife, and grasped it in her left hand, trying to angle it to cut the ropes with little success. Artemis whined, and she stopped. Dropping the knife, she sat between it and the curtain, just in time for it to part.

Boss's face appeared. He scowled as he looked her over, then unlocked the gate. Reaching a hand in, he tossed her two small packages.

"I told that fool Barry he could leave you these before, the idiot must have forgot. Keep quiet. You know what we'll do if you make trouble for us. Eat fast. I'll send Barry to retie the gag. That idiot should have left it on."

Boss locked the door and hung the curtain, his angry footsteps echoing as he walked away. With a sigh, Maia retrieved the packages, finding one was a bladder of stale, bitter water, and the other was a pie. Not even close to the quality of the one Barry's brother had made, the meat had a strong smell of spices used to cover the rancid tang of the meat. Even so, she was hungry, and thirsty. So she shared both with Artemis, and then returned to the knife.

Working at it for several minutes, Maia found she was unable to get sufficient pressure to cut the ropes by holding the knife. So she dropped it, then pushed it across the floor to the wire wall. Careful not to cut her hands, she propped the knife handle into the wire, holding the blade upright, along the ground. She placed her wrists on either side of the blade and moved them back and forth to saw through the ropes.

Just as she cut through the last of them, she heard noises outside and sat again to hide the knife. The curtain parted, and Barry's face appeared. He was wobbly, and maia could smell the drink on his breath. He opened the gate and stumbled in.

Rushing towards her, he covered her mouth before she could scream. Artemis reacted angrily, growling and snarling as she bit at his legs. The brute ignored the bites completely.

"No noise, or else it's over, girly!" he snarled as he dragged her away from the wall and fumbled at her arms.

Maia saw a flash of shiny metal as he hauled her hand

up. He stopped, staring at her hand, held aloft as the other hung by her side.

"Resourceful little bitch aren't you?" he said, then chuckled. "I guess I didn't need to risk this after all. I even forgot to give you food and water so I'd have an excuse to come down here later, and boss found me out. He was angry, but took it as me being an idiot, so we got away with it. He even sent me to retie the gag!"

"What are you talking about?" Maia whispered in a hissing voice. "And keep it down."

"Sorry Girly," Barry whispered back. "I told you we all have our roles to play, and I play mine. But I won't let it curse my soul. One day, I'd like to have a normal life, like my brother. When I told him about you, it was the angriest I've ever seen him. He made me promise to free you. He said if I didn't try, he'd never let me settle there."

"So your brother told you to? Is that why?"

"No!" Barry said, a little too loud. "But he made it clear I have to. I was already going to, if I could figure a way. You remind me of my little sister, may she rest. He was the one suggested the plan, and then Boss ruined it. I thought it was over, but boss is drinking now. I can't hang around for long. Must have taken ages to cut those ropes with that little knife against the wall."

Barry knelt on one knee and with a quick action cut the ropes around Maia's ankles. He stood, and walked to the gate.

"Do me a favour, smash the lock when you leave. I'm not latching it, but it has to look like you escaped without my help. Wait an hour at least."

"I've got more help than I need already," Maia said, smiling at him for the first time. "Thanks, Barry. I won't forget what you've done tonight."

He smiled back, his drunken face showing true compassion as he turned to leave.

"Wait, Barry," Maia said, rushing to hug him. "I'm sorry, I was so scared of you, it isn't fair on you to be just a scary thug. I want you to know you are way better than that. Go to your brother and settle. You can play that role instead of this one."

Barry hugged her briefly, and pushed her away. He smiled at her, then walked out of the pen, pulling the gate closed, and not latching it.

"I think I'll do that, as soon as I can free myself from Boss. Thanks, Girly." he whispered, before staggering away.

Maia sat, Artemis whining for comfort as she lay her head in her master's lap. She patted the dog gently as she relaxed, feeling some confidence in her situation for the first time.

"An hour?" Maia mused as she yawned. "I wonder if there will be long enough? I hope I can get away."

Carousing voices drifted to the pen from somewhere nearby, getting louder and more raucous as the time drew on. She could hear their intoxication in the laughter and shouting.

The adrenaline she felt at her pending escape kept her awake. She was thankful of that, because she was so tired now. But she knew she had to keep awake for a while longer. Maybe she could find a safe place to rest later.

After what felt like an eternity, she stood, and went to the gate. As she opened the gate, the curtain flew aside and a woman rushed in.

The stranger looked around, her eyes settling on the cut ropes on the ground, then at Maia, who was backing away nervously, ready to fight.

"Good, you've got some fight left," the woman said. "Quickly now, Alex told me everything."

"where is he?" Maia asked.

"Right here!" Alex said as he opened the horses pen.

"What are you doing over there?" Maia asked.

"You're taking my horse," the woman explained. "You need to be faster than on foot. If these bastards chase you, I want you to have a good head start."

"Will they chase us?"

"Yes. If you leave the dog, they'll have a harder time of it."

"Why? And no, Artemis comes with me."

"I thought as much," the woman said with a sigh. "That means they can claim somebody stole the dog. That will get them help from the other merchants, even if they don't mention they were selling a girl. But it can't be helped. It's your dog. Just be careful. If they catch you, run. Leave the dog if you have to. I'll buy it so we can get it back to you somehow."

While they were talking, Alex had placed a saddle and bridal on the horse, and led it out of the pen.

"Maia, walk on the left of the horse, between it and the wall. That way you're less likely to be seen. And carry Artemis."

"OK, but one of them came to free me. We have to break the lock so he isn't found out."

As Maia picked up Artemis, struggling for a moment to find balance with the weight of the dog in her arms, the woman picked up Alex's knife, jammed it into the lock, and wrenched it down hard. The blade snapped, and there was a pinging noise inside the latch mechanism.

"That should do, now get moving. We need to be fast."

Maia rushed from the pen, and walked between the horse and the wall, Artemis held by her rear, front paws and head on Maia's shoulder. She keep looking at the creature as they made their way past dozens of animal pens.

"Left here," Alex said. "We're going the long way around, but we have to leave the market by the right exit to avoid people. China Town is busy with the merchants tonight, so we have to keep to the far side of Paddy's to avoid your kidnappers possibly seeing us. Even if they're drunk, they'll still be dangerous."

After a slow walk around two full sides of the enormous building, they reached an exit. A sign over the doorway announced it as "Quay St."

"I have to leave you both here," the woman said. "Alex, look after the girl. I'll see you when you return. If you don't get back tomorrow, just come home dear. Your father and I will be waiting."

Alex hugged his mother, holding her for a long moment before leading the horse to the door.

"Wait, girl," the woman said. "One other thing. As long as you're in the city, stay out of the tunnels. The gangs that hide in them will be far worse than the group you've just escaped. And remember, just run. Leave the dog if you have to."

"Thank you, for everything," Maia said. "I've had so much help already since I got here. I'll try not to let it be wasted."

The woman smiled, waved at her son, and rushed back inside the darkened building. Maia rushed to Alex, who held out his hand. She looked at it, confused.

"Put the dog down. She'll follow you, right?"

"Yes," Maia said, putting Artemis on the ground and taking his hand.

"Now put your other hand on the saddle, step your right foot into the stirrup, here, and pull yourself up."

Maia tried to do as he said, and fell backwards. Patiently, he caught her, steadied her, and had her do it again. On the third try, she was up, and swung her left leg over, to sit straddling the huge creature.

Artemis stared at her master, confused. Alex flew into position behind her, his agility taking Maia by surprise. She looked down at the dog beside them.

"Artemis, follow," Maia said as the horse lurched forward, taking the stairs out to the street with little effort. Alex used the reigns to guide the horse left, and they made their way alongside the building for a short distance before turning into the grounds of a concrete jungle where a worn sign read "UTS."

The sounds of the drinking merchants soon were lost to the distance as they wandered through the empty city. Maia was stunned by the enormity of the buildings, the lack of any real trees, and the general dirtiness of the place.

"This place," she mumbled. "It's unbelievable."

"This is your first time seeing it?" Alex asked.

"Yeah..."

"Can you imagine what it must have been like?" he replied. "I mean, in the old times."

"I really can't," Maia said. "I can barely imagine it now, even though I'm seeing it for myself."

"Six million people lived here, before the end. Now,

about ten thousand, my dad says, scattered throughout the greater metropolitan area. All the old buildings just sit here. The people left scavenge for things to trade, and protect their territories violently, so we have to be careful where we go."

"Do you know their territories?"

"A little. We'll find our way to The Rocks. It's not a long way, but they'll have a hard time finding us. There is an old museum on George st and I know the people who control the area. it will be safe for the night."

"I hope you're right," Maia replied, stifling a yawn.

It was a little more than a half hour, and Alex directed the horse inside a building, and climbed down. He held a hand out for her, and helped her down as well.

"We'll be safe in here," he said. "I know it seems like we didn't go far, but if they look for us, they'll be looking in an awful lot of old buildings to find us."

Chapter 9 – Wandering

Alex woke Maia before sunrise. He had already taken the horse outside and left it grazing on a wide open grassy area next to the museum.

"The horse is grazing in First Fleet Park, next door. We should get him and head for the highway. I'd like to cross the harbour bridge before the merchants wake up and start searching for us."

Maia nodded, and stood, looking around. Artemis was laying nearby, and raised her head to watch.

"It's a shame, I would have liked to search this place a bit. It's probably got some interesting artefacts."

"There are plenty of places with things you would find interesting. For now, we should focus on getting you out of the city. Or at least as far from the merchants as possible. Once things are settled, perhaps you can come back to the city one day."

"Uncle always told me it was too dangerous to come here. But if I had you showing me around, I think we'd be fine."

"Uncle?"

"He was my teacher, and mentor, in the village. He had solar panels on his house and still has working devices from the old times. Music players, computer things with libraries of writing and pictures from back then, all sorts of things. He's always looking for more, but he is trying to get things like old books because he worries about the time when his electrical supply fails."

"In that case, if we get a chance, we'll find some saddle bags or something and you can take some books from somewhere."

"Artemis, come," maia said, following Alex out of the building. "I should find myself some kind of pack anyway. I'm going to need to get food for the journey, for me and for Artemis."

"That's true. If you have to travel into the mountains, you need to be prepared," Alex said. "I mean, sure you live there, but that doesn't mean you won't get lost. And getting lost in the mountains will get you killed, my dad says."

"Your dad is right," Maia said. "But if I can get to Windsor, I know my way from there pretty well."

"Windsor? That's a town on the western edges of the city, isn't it? I think I've heard of it."

"Yes, it's a pretty major town in our region. Still, it takes several days walking with the dogs to pull the cart."

They had reached the horse, and Alex helped her up, then swung up behind her before talking again.

"These dogs, were they all like Artemis?"

"Yes. The same breed. White swiss shepherds, my dad said. He told me they are all descended from a group of dogs which were taken to the village when they first started it up. They came from a place called Eishund."

"I've never heard of a town with that name," Alex said.

"I don't think it's a town. I think it was a place that bred the dogs though."

"Oh I see, so that was the kennel in the old times? It would be interesting if you could find the records – proper kennels were registered in those days, and they kept track of the breeding programs. Just like our horses."

"Does your family breed horses?"

"Not like the old days. We just have a couple, but in our area to the south west of the city, which is called Picton, there are a few people these days who do breed them. They're valuable animals, and rare."

"Yet your mother let us take this one instead of selling it?"

"My mum will always give everything for a girl in need. She had a cousin kidnapped once, and nobody helped her. My mother says she tries to do the right thing, so other people will learn to as well one day."

They reached the edge of the park, and found a break in the ancient fence, concealed in the long grasses. The horse gingerly pushed through onto a crumbling paved footpath, then out onto George St. Maia looked both ways, staring down the unlit street in the predawn. There was no sign of life.

"This street would have been busy in the old times, with their motorised vehicles backed up for miles." Alex said. "The locals burn away the grasses which try to take over."

"It's hard to imagine," Maia replied. "I mean, sure the place is huge, and all these buildings must have been built for somebody..."

"But so many people is unbelievable?" Alex finished for her.

"Yeah..." Maia said, pointing at a raised roadway to their immediate left. "You said we cross a bridge. Is that it?"

"No, that's one of the old highways. See the sign on the side? Cahill Expressway. It goes into a tunnel nearby, and you remember what my mum told you, I hope."

"Stay out of tunnels?"

"That's right. At this hour, the tunnels will all be occupied. Going into one and waking up the locals will not end well."

"Yeah, I can imagine."

"It's a shame, because that tunnel is the easiest way for us to get onto a road out of the city. I even know some people in that tribe, which is why I felt safe in the museum last night. But knowing somebody is never permission to invade their home unannounced. We can't afford that."

Alex turned the horse under the raised road, then turned to follow it away from the park and museum.

"Why would they choose to live in a tunnel instead of one of these buildings?" Maia asked.

"Ease of movement. The tunnels are all on major roads. Setting up a camp inside the tunnel allows them total control of who passes into their territory through them."

"So they live in tunnels instead of nice buildings..." Maia mused. "I still don't get it."

"Oh, not everybody is in tunnels. But a section of each group in the city does. And a lot of the buildings are too hard to live in. The stairs are ridiculous, so they only live in the lower floors, and a lot of them are really difficult for um..."

He hesitated, and Maia became impatient.

"Difficult for what?" she demanded.

"Um... Bathroom stuff. If the plumbing is shot, there's nobody who can fix it. The old sewerage systems, not all of them can still operate a century after the power went out."

Maia thought about that for a moment, then realised the mess they'd be left to deal with.

"Ohhh," she said. "So the buildings which are occupied, what do they do?"

"Usually they have water tanks on higher levels, fed from the roof when it rains, and people have refitted lower levels to receive that water, and flush the sewerage out into the city's drains."

"Is that safe?" Maia asked. "What about diseases and the smell?"

Alex turned the horse left, following a sign which read "Harrington Street."

"Remember, the population is tiny compared to the old times," Alex said. "What do you do in the village? I assume you have something like we use at home."

"Septic systems. We have to pump them out regularly, and the smell is awful. It fertilises the lands downhill from us, my dad jokes every time. We try to do it when the rain will help wash it away but that's not always possible."

"That sounds pretty bad," Alex said. "Sorry, it just does. At home we have big tanks on carts, and we pump the septic into those then take it away. I never thought to ask where it goes."

"I know it sounds bad," Maia said. "We've dug channels to guide it downhill and away from us. It's pretty revolting, really. Thankfully we have a good water reservoir uphill from the village so we can flush the channels properly."

They reached an intersection at Essex St, where a child ran away from them and into a strange shaped small grey building. To Maia, it looked out of place, the other three corners being tall but this one looked nothing like those, with sloping roof following the hillside as Essex st ran down towards the next intersection.

"I'd be totally lost on my own," Maia mumbled. "This place is so confusing!"

"Which is why I came along," Alex said. "But we should get moving, we don't know who that kid lives with and if they know your merchant thieves, it could be bad for us. Even if they don't, the less people who can say they saw us, the better."

They moved on, and soon reached the next intersection at Grosvener Street, where they turned right. They followed that way uphill, passed another intersection, then followed the road as it passed a third. It continued under a raised road, and turned right alongside the ancient structure to run parallel to it, uphill until they met to become merely lanes of the same immense thoroughfare.

Maia's jaw dropped at the expanse of crumbling tarmac. It was like eight roads crammed into one, wide enough to hold a small village, and the tarmac stretched out before them like a weathered stone parkland, inviting them on.

Tumbling steel gantries draped across the road up ahead, the worn signs barely legible after a century and then some of weather. The wind whipped at their hair as they made their way cautiously out into the open expanse.

Alex kicked the horse's sides, and spurred it into a trot. Maia gasped and grabbed hold of the pommel on the saddle, struggling for a moment to stay on. Artemis ran alongside, darting out into the open space and back again a few times, sniffing the ground with curiosity and wonder.

To the east, the sun was finally rising, and the sky took on an orange glow. In the distance, two stone pillars and a massive metal structure between them came into view.

"What's that?" Maia asked.

"The harbour bridge. It was a famous landmark in the old times."

"With the size of this road, I can see why," Maia replied. "And that's the way we're going?"

"It's the best way out of the city for us," he replied.

"We can get out without using the tunnels, and I can probably get you to Windsor then head south to go home."

"That sounds good. I hope it all works out," she said, doubt in her tone.

"You worry too much," Alex said. "Don't worry, you'll be fine."

"I'm causing you a lot of trouble..."

"Don't worry about that right now. Until we're over the bridge, there is a risk of discovery. If anybody sees us, they could tell the merchants where to look."

"They don't guard the bridge like the tunnels?"

"Not like the tunnels, but there's probably somebody on lookout, somewhere up there," he said, looking up as they approached the bridge. "Once we're across we need to follow the left lanes to the Pacific Highway. That way we avoid the next big tunnel and can hopefully get ourselves moving in the right direction."

They paused on the centre of the bridge, to gaze at the sunrise over the harbour. There was not a sign of humanity, aside from the legacy of steel, glass and concrete they travelled through. Maia shuddered.

"What is it?" Alex asked.

"This place, it's eerie. It feels haunted."

"It does," he replied, and spurred the horse back into motion. "We should keep moving."

They rode on, over the remainder of the bridge, and true to his word, Alex guided them left, to follow a beaten sign which announced the Pacific Highway.

"The buildings are still so huge," Maia marvelled. "How many people must have suffered when the old times ended?"

"That's why it feels haunted. Because we know they died, millions of them. And a lot of them fled as well. A lot of people still fear the city because of that."

Soon the buildings did begin to get smaller, and Maia began to feel more comfortable with the surroundings when they saw the first houses, with wide open yards out the front. The yards were unkempt and overgrown, but they took the opportunity to stop, stretching their legs and letting the horse graze for a short while out the front of an ancient red brick building.

Curious about the building, Maia looked around, and near the corner of the grassed area found a sign. She could make out the letters s, c, h and o, but the rest of it was too badly worn for an explanation.

"It's an old school," Alex said as he came to stand beside her.

"I'm getting hungry," Maia said. "What will we do for food?"

"You never even noticed the saddle bag, did you?"

"The what?"

"My mother gave us a couple of days supplies in a bag. It's on the back of the saddle. And it looks like Artemis will help out as well."

"Artemis? What?" Maia said, looking around for the pup, who was scratching at something under the low branches of a nearby tree.

"She's found some rabbits. That would be an entry to their burrow. If we catch one, it will feed all three of us for a day if we don't eat like pigs."

"We don't have rabbits in the mountains."

"Don't worry, they're everywhere at Picton. I catch them for food all the time. I can skin and gut it in five minutes. Artemis will love the meat."

Suddenly, the dog pounced, and barked. Looking up at Maia as she ran over. Artemis had the animal held beneath her front paws, wriggling desperately to escape. Without stopping to think if the dog would mind, Alex dove forward and snatched the rabbit up.

"I'll give it back," he said to Artemis, who growled, not wanting to release the prize.

"Artemis! Leave it," Maia snapped, and the dog backed down, watching Alex with jealous eyes as he scooped the wriggling rabbit up, before snapping its neck in a fluid motion.

Alex knelt on the ground and pulled out a knife, effortlessly cutting off the head and slipping the blade under the skin. With a ripping sound, he removed the skin in a single piece then set about gutting it.

"She'll eat raw meat, right?" Alex asked.

"Of course," Maia said. "Though I'm not sure I could watch you do that again. That little guy was adorable."

"Adorable or not, he's still food," Alex quipped as Artemis reached in to sniff at the offal on the ground. "Artemis, leave that."

Standing, Alex shook the carcass downwards in a rapid motion, shaking the blood and remaining entrails into the grass, before tossing the meat to the pup.

"There you go, Artemis, eat up. You'll need the energy. We've got rations for us, but not for you."

"How did you learn to do that?"

"We do what we have to to live," Alex replied. "Don't you have meat in the village?"

"We have chickens. But my family are the traders, so we don't have anything much to do with the butchering side of things."

Alex fetched rations, and they ate quietly, Artemis tearing at the meat with relish, while Maia wondered what other surprises the day had in store.

Chapter 10 – Pursuit?

Greg was welcomed into a the militia and went with a small group to search for clues as to the whereabouts of Maia and those who abducted her. They journeyed for days, wandering the countryside in search of clues.

The militia had a clear understanding of the country, and knew where the bandit gangs tended to roam, so they headed south then west, and eventually arrived in Blackheath, atop the mountains.

One of the militia directed Greg to a bakery, and he went in search of lunch.

"Welcome," said a man wearing an apron.

"Hi, I'm here with the Windsor Militia. We were just looking for some lunch."

"Who's your commander?"

"Daryl, I'm not sure of his surname, if he has one."

"I know Daryl. OK, How many of you are there?"

"Seven of us, myself included."

"Seven pies it is then," the baker said. "I'll give you the potato topped ones, Daryl likes those."

The man set about packaging the food, pausing briefly to look at Greg.

"I haven't seen you before. Are you new to the militia?"

"Yes. I'm not really a member. I'm accompanying them while I look for somebody."

"Oh, I see," the baker said. "Do you mind if I ask who?"

"I'm from Gospers. Our trade girl was abducted on her way to Windsor. They took all the trade goods and abducted her. The militia think those responsible may have come this way."

"They did," the baker said.

"They did?" Greg asked, suddenly alert. "Are you sure?"

"Yes. My brother, he's a good man, but he's involved with a dangerous group. He was with them, and he spoke to me about the girl. He intends to try to free her in the City. Hopefully without the others knowing."

"Why the city?"

"That's where they're going, to sell her. Here's your lunch. If the Militia catch them, go easy on Barry. Tell Daryl it's a favour to me."

"Thanks. I'll pass all that on," Greg said, grabbing the pies and heading for the door.

The baker coughed, and Greg stopped. He turned back and the baker had his hand out. Greg put the pies back on the counter.

"Oh, of course, I'll fetch Daryl for some money."

"Don't worry about it," The baker said. "If you haven't got it on you, take the food, I'll send the invoice to the militia in Windsor with the next trader."

"Thank you," Greg said, taking the food and walking out to find the militia.

*   *   *

The rations finished, Maia and Alex wandered the over grown school, leaving Artemis to eat the rabbit. The horse had wandered from where they had entered the grassy area to the far end of the premises, where it was grazing out of site of the sign post where they had been.

"There must be a library somewhere, if it's a school," Maia said. "I'd like to see what I can find there."

"Will Artemis wander off?"

"No, I think she's quite settled where she is for the moment," Maia said.

They walked around the building until they found a door. It was closed, but badly weathered. Alex kicked it, and it fell ajar. Maia squeezed in first, Alex following.

A foyer greeted them, dank and mouldy. Through an open doorway, a long corridor led to the rear of the building. Maia entered the corridor, not having any real notion of where they were going. They passed room after room, each one lined with dust covered desks and chairs.

The dust and mildew lent the hallways a peculiar smell, and the detritus of decades upon decades of storms blowing leaves and the like into the many broken windows gave it a feeling of being more outside than in.

Dampness had ruined many sections of wall and ceiling alike, and they soon came to realise it was a dangerous place to enter thanks to the risk of collapse.

To the left at the far end of the corridor, double doors stood open. On one were the letters "LIBR," and the other "ARY."

"This is it," Maia said, not believing how easy it was to find.

She walked in, to find the room dark, with the few windows covered by weathered wooden panels. She tripped over something and looked down, wondering what it might be. It was hard to see in the darkness.

"Just a minute," Alex said, striding to one of the boarded windows and wrenching the panel away. Even with the passage of time and the decay of the wood, it wasn't an easy task, but with much grunting and twisting, it came free, causing a bright shaft of sunlight to stream in from outside.

"Oh!" Maia gasped, her hand flying up to cover her mouth as she stared, eyes wide, at the thing she had tripped over.

A rotting strip of fabric, which looked like it had once resembled a long skirt, was draped over some bones. They were long, and as her eyes followed them, she found they ended at the worn leather of an old shoe.

"She was young," Alex said. "The poor girl. She must have been here when the people all left. Perhaps it was a boarding school or something and she had no way to go home?"

"We can't just leave her here," Maia said.

"We can try to bury her, but we don't have any tools to do it. She's been here for a long time."

"There might be something here," Maia said.

"There might be, but those sort of tools would probably have been in a shed outside. It's likely they were taken a long time ago."

"I guess you're right," Maia said. "If we can find something, we can deal with her."

"What do you suppose killed her?" Alex asked.

"Probably one of the viruses that went through the city," Maia said. "Uncle told me there were loads of them. The end wasn't a sudden thing, and the climate was changing as well. Could have been anything. She might have even starved. At the height of the bad times, they had trouble growing food all over the place. There wasn't enough water and the heat killed things faster than they could plant them over the summer months, and the frosts and storms ruined crops in the colder months as well."

"Sounds like a pretty scary time."

Maia walked away, gazing at shelves of crumbling books as she walked around the library. Along one wall, old screens sat in front of uncomfortable looking chairs.

"Computers," she mumbled as she idly pressed a button on one, knowing it wasn't going to start up before she even touched it, but feeling she had to try anyway.

"Hey, what's this?" Alex called from behind a counter where he was rummaging in a cupboard.

He took out an old leather satchel and placed it on the counter. He started pulling things out of the bag. A cable with a funny box thing attached in the middle, a box with several shiny discs in it, and a folding device.

"It's a computer," Maia said as she joined him at the counter. "And a bunch of discs. Can I see?"

He handed her the box of discs and she wiped the dust from the box. The writing proclaimed the disks to be "The Encyclopedia Britannica." Maia opened the computer and pressed the power button. It was similar to the device at Uncles, if a little older. Nothing happened.

"Battery's dead," she said, closing it and packing it all back into the bag.

"So it's useless?" Alex asked.

"Not necessarily, it might just need to have power connected. I'm going to take it with me."

She put the shoulder strap of the satchel over her arm and turned away, carrying the bag as she walked back towards where she had been. Just then, Artemis began barking, rapid and angry. She ran to the opened window, and looked out. Alex joined her.

From their vantage point, they could see to the corner, where several men were approaching from the road.

"Run!" Alex said as he raced from the room. "Get to the horse and get out of here. Don't worry about Artemis, I'll find you. If you get caught here, it's over."

In spite of the urgency, she couldn't bare to leave Artemis, and watched as one of the men reached her, grabbing viciously at the pup's scruff. The animal snarled and lunged, but the man dodged and prepared to kick the dog, just as Alex ran up to him and shoved the man away. With one leg raised, the man tumbled to the ground and Alex scooped Artemis up protectively.

"You little bastard," the man growled. "So you're the brat who stole that dog from the market. We'll have your hide, boy!"

"I never stole the dog," Alex said. "I just got it to trust me by feeding it meat. That's how I got it away from that girl who stole our horse."

"Your horse?" one of the men snarled, striding forward.

"Careful Boss," the fallen man said. "He might be armed."

"No, he's just a brat. And I don't trust him. That child over the bridge saw a boy and a girl on a horse together. The boy is telling lies. Where's the girl?"

"She got away, with my horse."

"I don't believe you," the man said.

"I don't care. The city militia don't take kindly to slave traders."

"And who's going to listen to you?" the man snarled, drawing a machete. "Nobody, once you're dead."

"You really think I'm the only one who knows the truth?" Alex snapped. "If I'm not back tonight, alive, the militia will be told everything. How you kidnapped that girl and planned to sell her. How this was her dog and you planned to sell it too. How you stole her trade goods and sold those."

"You're bluffing, kid."

"Am I? Do you think I managed to sneak a draft horse, a girl, and a dog out of those markets and out of the city without help? I'll pay you for the damn dog, but you let the girl go. And the horse goes with her. My Family will cope without it. And if you don't let me go, you're all done for. My mother knows who you are, who the girl is, and what you were planning. And she knows the chief guard at Paddy's well."

"Fine, you come back with us. But if we don't get paid for the dog, there'll be trouble."

"Oh, there'll be trouble alright," Alex snarled, walking away from the building, back towards the city. "You try anything at all, I'll have you all locked away for the rest of your miserable lives. And if you lay a finger on me, those lives will be short."

Maia had seen enough, she had to trust the boy to find her later. She ran out of the library and into the room opposite, then climbed out a window and found the horse, grazing nearby. Securing the satchel to the saddle, she climbed onto the horse, and pulled the reins, turning it to continue the journey away from the city.

She stayed off the road as much as she could, trying to remain out of site of the men, until it took a left hand turn and she was able to ride in the open again.

Artemis was gone. Maia wept, the pup who had stayed by her side all this time might be lost forever. The tears grew as she rode. And she let them fall.

"Arty..." she muttered, over and over, as the horse trotted away from the pup she had raised.

"Alex, you damn well better keep your word," she shouted finally, after some twenty minutes of a breaking heart, not caring who heard her.

*   *   *

Greg's breath came heavily as he jogged, fighting to keep up the pace set by the militia men from Windsor. The way was mostly downhill, but the uphill sections were harrowing. They had picked up the pace, now that they had a lead on the girl. It seemed these militia were taking the situation seriously.

The road to Blackheath had been a long hard climb, but returning from it was an easier thing, even at a run. It troubled him that their prey had a five day head start. If the man who had said he planned to free the girl failed, Greg may never reach her in time.

"What are our chances?" Greg asked between gasps as he rushed to catch Daryl, leading the pack.

"If she hasn't been freed, or somehow escaped?" Daryl said. "Slim, but not zero. If we can find the men responsible, we may be able to learn where she has gone, who they sold her to. Without that information, we're out of luck. The kinds of men who buy girls don't keep them in a way that would let us know where they are."

Greg was quiet for a long time after that, but he ran on, ignoring the distress of his body, determined to keep his promise to a friend.

Chapter 11 – The Hotel

Maia rode into the afternoon, following the same road as it wound its way through endless miles of abandoned suburbs. The buildings grew larger, then smaller, then larger again. Even the smallest of them seemed huge to her eyes.

But Maia wasn't paying a lot of attention to her surroundings anymore. She was simply sticking to the road, following signs that said Pacific in the name, and hoping it was the right direction.

She worried about how much time they had wasted at the library, but she was thankful that Alex had seemingly led the enemy away. She was free to take as long as she needed. Though she was still concerned that she needed his knowledge of the city surrounds, however limited that might have been.

Maia had never imagined so many buildings, so many roads. She would become completely lost in short order if she wandered the wrong way. This was more confusing and dangerous to her than all the dark forest of the mountains.

Slowing, Maia approached a large intersection where the pacific highway passed over another large road, which emerged from a tunnel. Nervous, she crossed, but saw nobody. Up ahead, a strange building sat, with a large open area under a roof with no walls, several strange boxes spaced out underneath it. A weathered sign bore only two letters. "BP."

Climbing down from the horse, she tied it to the sign and walked to the building. She had seen these places in the films Uncle sometimes showed her on the folding computer. They had something to do with ancient vehicles, like the SUV.

She knew from the films these buildings had useful things inside. The glass doors were smashed, tattered fabric screens behind glass shards which hung from the remains of a fragile film of tinting.

Careful to avoid getting cut, Maia pushed through the doorway and entered the building. It was long since ransacked, and spoiled goods were spilled from glass fronted closets along the back wall.

Racks divided the floor space into aisles, and there were still some goods on display, presumably not found useful by those who had come here over the years.

A rack on the same wall as the door held a number of square plastic cases sealed in disintegrating plastic film. She picked one up, and looked at it, turning it over in her hands. The film crumbled away, and the text visible beneath it said "Peter Allen."

"I know this name," she murmured, "The man who sang that song. I remember Uncle telling me his name. So these must contain music."

She pulled and pried at the plastic case, until it burst open in her hands, spilling a disc to the floor. She immediately recognised it as the same shape as the ones in the Encyclopedia Britannica box.

"These must all be music then. And I could likely play them on that folding computer if I ever make it work."

She scooped up an armful of the plastic cases and carried them outside. Walking to the horse, she crammed as many as she could into the satchel holding the computer from the library, then returned to the building to see if there was anything else there she could use.

Entering the building she walked to the far end, where a sturdy counter blocked her path, a solid door to the end. Steel cables, strung tight, prevented her accessing the area behind, though they had long ago darkened with corrosion.

Pulling at the cables, she found she couldn't make a space wide enough to get through, and the steel door miraculously was still in reasonable order even after a century of neglect. Maia guessed the owners of the building probably kept anything of real value behind that door, and it might still be there.

For some time, Maia investigated the counter. Peering through, she pulled at cables, trying to see if anything in there was worth taking. Then she caught a glimpse of a book, tucked behind the wall at the end of the counter furthest from the door. It was a long way from where she could squeeze an arm in, but rested on the counter, taunting her.

Maia's curiosity was piqued. It looked like a big book, and though it was dusty, it looked dry, as if its position on the counter top had protected it from much of the weather. She pushed her arm in as far as she could, and felt just the tips of her fingers brush the pages. It was tantalising, and infuriating.

She could feel the brittleness of the paper just from running her fingers over the edges of the pages. Maia knew that even if she secured the book, the pages may simply crumble in her hands. Yet she was determined. She turned away from the counter and looked around the room. Some of the racks had a bar across the front, as if to stop products from falling. She went to the nearest one and grasped it, pulling and twisting, but to no avail.

Then she investigated the shelves themselves, and noticed that were held up on long brackets which hooked into a frame. She kicked the underside of a shelf and it flew up and away from the rack, leaving a long bracket swinging from the hooks at its end. Grasping the bracket, she hefted it upwards, and removed it from the frame.

With a smile, she took the bracket and passed it through the metal cables. She used it to carefully drag the ancient book closer, before picking it up and reverently removing it, through the cables, to hold it like a treasure.

Carrying the book outside, Maia looked at it in the light, the dust hard to remove, and the plastic cover protecting it yellowed with age. She rubbed with her hands, and tilted the book to read the cover, speaking the words aloud.

"UBD Gregory's," She read. "2020 Street Directory, Sydney and Blue Mountains. What on earth is this?"

Carefully, she opened the book to a random page. Her eyes lit up. She closed the book, then walked back to the horse, more than happy with the find.

"Maps," she said, smiling as she stashed it in the saddle bag, filling the space the rations had taken previously. "This is a great find. I just have to try to keep it from falling apart. For now I'll stick to the Pacific Highway, like Alex told me, but if I get lost, that book might save me."

With a clumsy, awkward effort Maia climbed onto the horse. She pulled the reins as she had seen Alex do, and directed it back to the road. As she continued away from the city, the buildings were smaller again now. But the road remained enormous compared to anything she was used to.

Even in its crumbling weathered state, the Pacific Highway impressed her. An army could march on its width, she surmised as she rode. Maia felt she was making good time as she continued, passing endless old buildings and weathered signs, being sure to keep to the same road.

Then she reached a large intersection, and on the left hand corner opposite her, she saw a group of people seated outside an ancient two story brick building. The weathered sign proclaimed the building to be "The Great Northern Hotel." A woman stood and waved at Maia,

"Horse woman, where are you travelling?" the woman shouted.

"I hope to reach Windsor," Maia replied, not wishing to give further detail than that. "Is this the right way?"

"It's the long way around, for sure, but if you take a left at Wahroonga, you should get there. Eventually. You'll need to take the old M2 then the A2, but you'll make it that way. Probably smart anyway, if you'd gone straight down the M2, there are some less friendly types controlling that route."

"Thank you, I'll watch for the signs," Maia replied, spurring the horse to continue on.

"Wait," the woman said. "It's a long ride, and you've not got a lot of daylight left. Why not camp here with us for the night, and continue on in the morning? We'll give you a good feed, and I'd like to hear the story of a girl as young as you travelling alone on a horse. I'm sure it's quite the tale."

"I don't know..." Maia said.

"Look," the woman persisted. "There are a lot of

unsavoury people out there, but I promise you, we live here, and we're good people. We provide what help we can to travellers, and in return, they trade whatever they have we might find value in. Would you feel safer if it was a proper transaction? You got anything we might like? Our rooms are comfortable, and the kitchen is the finest in the region."

Maia still hesitated, while the woman approached. She wore an apron, and had a motherly air as she came closer.

"Listen, child, I have kids, I know your mother must be worried for you. I'd feel better if I knew somebody was watching out for them. So stay with us. I promise you won't be robbed. We're honest people running an honest business and trading with travellers who come through. My husband is on a trading trip to Windsor now, else he'd be here to greet you too.".

"You trade to Windsor?"

"Yes. We find the foods are better from Windsor, and the prices we get for our things are better too."

"What do you trade?"

"Devices and items fetched from the area. Look around yourself child. There are scarcely any people left in the city, but buildings aplenty, all full of the old goods. Also, my husband makes whisky using supplies grown around Windsor. Our visitors all seem to enjoy his drink. I'm not a whisky drinker myself."

"Do you have electricity?" Maia asked.

"Yes, we have an old wind generator and a battery. It powers lights and some small devices."

"Can you play these?" Maia asked, fetching one of the disks from the satchel.

"No, but if you have a device in that bag which can, we could power it. If you treat us to hearing whatever music is on those disks tonight, we can count that as payment."

"I don't know if the device works," Maia said.

"Well child, if it doesn't, would you part with some of the disks? We can trade them to another traveller, there is bound to be somebody interested in them."

"OK then," Maia said, accepting the woman's hand

and dismounting. "I'm Maia, by the way."

"I'm Wendy," the woman said. "My word, you do look like you need a feed. When did you last have a proper meal?"

Maia blushed, looking down, fighting not to let her emotion and her exhaustion show. Wendy touched Maia's chin, tilting her face upwards and looking at her with genuine concern.

"We can't have that, child. You must have been through a lot. Come, I'll get you a real feed. Nigel! See her horse gets stabled, fed and watered. Put her things in room twelve and let me know as soon as it's done."

"Yes, Ma'am," one of the men replied, rushing to take the horse and lead it to one end of the building as Wendy took Maia's hand and almost dragged her inside.

Maia sat on a stool at the end of a long kitchen as Wendy fussed about, cooking up a storm. The older woman was quiet, aside from concerned tutting as Maia explained everything which had happened, the catharsis of having somebody to talk to who was so motherly bringing her to tears as she reached the point where she lost Artemis.

Wendy stopped what she was doing and knelt in front of the girl, resting a hand on her shoulder and looking her in the eyes.

"Now child, you know he promised he'd find you. The pup will be returned to you, just have patience. That boy sounds like he's a good one. He'll be true to his word. Now then, do you mind? I've cooked enough for everyone, since it was nearly meal time anyway. If you could fetch the plates and take them to the long table through that door, I'll be right behind you with the food. Then we'll see what we can do about that music."

Maia nodded, fetched the stack of plates Wendy pointed to, and took them through to a long table. She placed them out around the table, and finished as Wendy came in with two large platters of steaming food.

"Nigel!" Wendy shouted. "You stabled that horse yet?"

"Yes Ma'am," Nigel replied, huffing as he ran into the room. "Just done hauling some hey in for the animal. She's a beauty of a horse, girl. You were lucky to get her."

"Good. Fetch the girl's satchel bag and bring it in here, would you?"

"Yes, Ma'am," Nigel replied, turning and leaving the room.

"Now then, before we get the rest of the food out and the cutlery, we'll get that device set up over here I think," Wendy said, dragging a small side table to where a tall lamp stood, bathing the room in a soft light. "This lamp is electric, of course, and it has a spare point for another device next to where it's connected. My Husband's grandfather first set it all up, and his father replaced the battery about a decade ago. We've been fortunate to have power here all these years."

Nigel returned, handing Wendy the satchel then standing back to watch, curious about the device inside. Wendy handed it to Maia. The girl opened the bag and piled thirteen discs in their cases on the side table, then took out the folding computer and its cable. Looking carefully, she found where the cable connected to the device and plugged it in, while Wendy took the other end and connected it to the outlet.

With trepidation, Maia pressed the power button. She shrieked with excitement when the device made a noise and writing appeared on the screen. It took several minutes to stop making a chirping noise, and the red light on its front to stop flashing, but when it had, the device was on the same screen, albeit with a few different icons, as the one at uncles she was used to.

"It works," Maia said, awe in her voice. "Uncle told me he found six dead ones before he got one to work."

"Uncle?" Wendy asked, eyebrow raised.

"He's like a teacher back home," Maia said.

"Not in Windsor he isn't," Wendy replied. "You mean in your home village? Oh well, if you're headed for Windsor, I believe you. We all trade to the bigger towns."

Fumbling around the sides of the device, Maia found a small button, and when she pressed it, a draw popped open. Fetching the disc which said "Peter Allen," she took it from the case and pushed it into the draw, then closed it. The device whirred and the screen changed, and then music began to play. Softly at first, but Maia had seen that screen at Uncles, so she knew what to do. She turned the volume to its fullest, and the music could be heard around the room.

"Marvellous!" Wendy exclaimed. "I so rarely get to hear the old songs. Thank you, Maia. Nigel, please call everybody in. It's time to eat, and drink, and enjoy some music, thanks to this girl."

Chapter 12 – Family

Maia slept well, better than she had in weeks, and in the morning. Wendy had her reunited with her horse, and on her way, all her possessions still with her, plus a few days food and water as a parting gift.

Wendy implored her to take care, and sat with her for several minutes, pouring over the maps in the book she had found the day before.

Together, they plotted the way to Windsor, and Maia felt more confident than ever that she was going to make it home. Wendy hugged Maia close before she mounted the horse, and stood waving until the hotel was out of site.

Maia sang as she rode, her smile broad and genuine, as she gazed in wonder at the world around her, so strange and yet so familiar. The many songs she had heard the night before were abuzz in her mind, and she sang what she could recall, humming where the words eluded her. Song after song, her spirits high and the streets deserted.

Brick houses and apartments dominated the scenery for a long while, with many gathered monoliths of concrete and broken glass rising from the landscape like haunted mountains amongst the sprawling houses and overgrown gardens.

Around mid morning, Maia paused, allowing the horse to graze in a grassed area. She sat and rested, her back against the enormous trunk of an ancient palm tree. The long grasses waved in the breeze as she fetched the book.

Searching through the maps, starting at the first page they had marked before using the index as Wendy had shown her, Maia located the hotel. She then followed the road along, counting the intersections and the turns, until she found the place she was now resting.

The book called it "Kenneth Slessor Park." Maia thought that sounded like a person's name, and she wondered briefly who Kenneth Slessor might have been.

What had Mr Slessor done that warranted a pocket of garden in this sprawling concrete maze to be named after him?

She made a mental note to find out who this man was, who's palm tree sheltered her, and what he had done to earn such an honour. Looking around, there was one of the tall ancient monoliths beside it on one side. On the other, in the direction she was headed, was a large open field of tarmac, with several ancient vehicles, battered by the weather, parked in a neat row.

Checking the horse was alright, Maia stood, and walked over to the vehicles. They were badly damaged. Something had long ago smashed the glass of their windows, and leaves, dirt and other rubbish had blown inside.

Some were shaped like the SUV she had ridden in the back of, and Maia was fascinated to see the differences when bandits hadn't stripped everything out. It must have taken a lot of effort to do what they had done.

Maia wanted to climb inside one, and feel what it was like to drive such a thing, but they felt somehow protected. As though the ghosts of the ancients still watched over their property, anxious that some thief drive them away forever.

She walked from one to the next, finding all in the same condition. But then, peering into the back seat of an SUV, she gasped, her hands flying to her face as she backed away in horror. There in the back, a strange capsule was strapped in, like a baby's cot. Maia leaned closer, inspecting the strange container. Within, tattered rags, hinting at once luxurious blankets hung morbidly over a tiny rib cage.

Turning, Maia ran from the dreadful scene, wailing in grief for the long dead child, taken from the world in such lonely isolation. Maia had always been keenly fascinated by history. But now...

If this was what the ancient times had brought to it's most precious, most vulnerable...

Why did she seek to learn from it? She suddenly felt she did not want to know what had happened – to the people, to the world, but most of all to that poor baby, locked away from the world, wrapped in blankets that would one day become a shroud, so morbid and terrible.

Maia vowed that no matter where she searched, she wouldn't go looking inside those ancient vehicles again. Reaching the palm tree, she planted both hands on it, and leaned their, wailing her grief to the wind.

*   *   *

Wendy waited till the girl was out of sight, then walked inside. Finding Nigel, she dragged him outside.

"Nigel," Wendy said, conspiratorially. "I'm worried for the girl."

"I am too, mistress," Nigel replied.

"Follow her. I hear talk of a group of settlers on the road ahead not allowing people through. I don't know their goals, but I beg you, protect that child."

"Yes, ma'am," Nigel said, and ran after Maia.

"Be safe, young one," Wendy muttered. "My dear brother would never forgive me if I let you come to harm."

*   *   *

After some time, Maia was back to her usual self. The Horse had stayed nearby, and watched her now, as she approached. Maia climbed onto the horse, and began the ride out of the park.

As she reached the road, and passed the vehicles, she could not stop herself from repeatedly glancing over at them, wishing there was some way of honouring the life of the child.

As she rode out of sight of the park and it's gruesome neighbour, that image of the child did not leave her thoughts. After an hour, she reached another area of greenery, one the book said was Regimental Park.

It was more overgrown than Kenneth Slessor park, but she felt she needed to walk a little, so she dismounted and led the horse into the long grass. Maia wandered aimlessly as she breathed in the smells of the grasses and shrubs which filled the area.

The park consisted of an embankment, topped by a low wall, and overgrown with grasses. It was difficult under foot, but wandering along the bottom of the embankment, Maia soon found a shallow culvert and followed it, reaching an open drainage channel. She climbed out of it and into a vast flat expanse.

It was scrub land, though she could tell at some point it had been manicured lawn. The area was flatter than any normal garden. Maia looked across the field and wondered what purpose it had held in ancient times. Turning away, she continued along the top of the embankment, on the safer, level ground over the wall.

After a while, she reached the corner of the park, and found wide, open and crumbled stairs back down to the street.

It was clear to Maia, from the state of this place, just how much time had passed since all the events which brought an end to the old times had occurred. Fires, floods, plagues of disease and vermin, countless events compiled into a long, slow death for the civilisation which had built this city she journeyed through.

Nothing she said or did could change what had happened, and nothing she felt or thought on seeing the things she saw would change the situation. She nodded, as if in company, and cemented her desire to continue the path she had chosen for her life. She would come to understand all there was to know about this world, if it took her the rest of her days.

Returning along the bottom of the embankment, she found the horse, and mounted it. Directing the horse back onto the road, she fetched a sandwich Wendy had provided from her bags, and ate it as the horse walked. There was a long journey ahead, but Maia realised now just how much more lay after this. Her larger journey would not begin until she had made it back to Gospers.

Forty five minutes later, she found another hotel. It bore a striking resemblance to the place she had stayed, with Wendy and her family, but appeared less hospitable.

It was in less favourable repair, and bore a sign which read "Green Gate Hotel." Maia chose not to stop and investigate. While the building seemed sturdy enough, windows were broken, and there was no sign of life within. It seemed a shame to Maia, and she wondered if someday a family would make a home of it, as Wendy and her group had done at the Great Northern Hotel.

Shortly thereafter, she was riding past a long brick wall, and she could see trees and gardens inside surrounding a large complex of residences. The place was large, larger than her own village, and offered security to anybody who chose to live there, even now.

She was staring at the first entrance, a sturdy, strangely well maintained gate, the first of at least three she could see as the wall ran alongside the road, into the distance. Maia was so distracted, she didn't notice the group approaching her.

"Hello," a male voice called, startling her out of her reverie.

Maia looked at them. There were four men, and a girl, she guessed about her own age. The girl was on a horse, smaller than Maia's, but no less impressive. The horse pulled a small cart, and the men were atop it.

"Hello," Maia said.

"It's strange to find a young lady travelling here. Where are you headed?" the man said.

"Windsor," Maia replied, too late seeing the girl's subtle head shake and worried expression.

"Windsor eh?" the man replied. "You'd be headed to the turn at Wahroonga then. You may want to avoid that route today. There's a fire down that way, and the groups in the area are all out fighting it. They don't usually get along, that lot, and likely won't take kindly to a stranger in the way."

"That sounds troublesome," Maia mused.

"Indeed," the man said. "Tell you what, how about you join our camp for the evening. We're in there."

Maia followed his pointing arm, which indicated the wall she had been staring at.

"Why would I stay with you?" she asked, as the gate opened and a woman came out.

"Oh good, you're back boys. Come along inside.

Hurry now,"

"That's the girl's Grandmother," the man said, drawing a startled look from the girl on the horse. "We're travellers from the west of the mountains. We found this place a few seasons ago, on a previous journey to the city. We've made use of it each journey since. Don't worry, it's perfectly safe."

"I'm not sure," Maia said. "The day is only half over, and I have far to go."

"As do we," the man replied. "but as I say, today is not a good time to take that road, and we never go from this place into the city without a full day ahead of us. There are too many delays, what with those tunnel gangs and the like."

"I suppose you make sense," Maia said. "If that is true. Then we can exchange notes about our roads ahead."

"Good, come now, you'll need to dismount to fit through the gate."

"Agreed," Maia said, climbing down as the girl did the same.

"Come, come child," the woman called, rushing forward to bustle the two girls into the gate.

Maia glanced back over her shoulder as she was ushered and shoved, worrying for the horse, and for her belongings. The girl clutched at her arm, pulling her along as they were herded along a path, the gardens thick and crowded along either side.

"I'm sorry," the girl whispered. "I really am. They took me the same way."

"What?" Maia said, louder.

"Keep quiet, you two," the woman snapped, jabbing her fingers into Maia's side, winding her. "You're our girls now, both of you. We need as many as we can find if this settlement is to last."

"Ma'am Boss," the man who had spoken said. "Shall we put her with this other one?"

"They can share a room for the time being," Ma'am Boss said. "It's good for a young girl to have a friend. It makes a forced marriage easier to bare. It's only a matter of time, and two of you men will have earned them for yourselves."

"Thank you, Ma'am boss," the man said.

Maia felt like vomiting. That man was hideous, near as old as Uncle, but with none of his charm or intellect. The rest looked no better. She felt a wave of bitter despair. The shocks of the day had her unsteady already, and the prospect of a man like this forcing himself upon her was more than she could bare.

Fortunately, at that moment a door into an apartment was opened, and the woman shoved her inside. The girl meekly followed, then the door slammed closed. Maia heard rusty locks securing them inside.

Maia sat on the ground and cried.

"I've really had enough today." she moaned.

"I'm truly sorry," the girl said. "My name's Elly. They kidnapped me about a year ago, and beat me senseless when I tried to escape."

"They won't beat me," Maia said, wiping her eyes and looking at the girl with steel in her expression.

"You mean to escape?" Elly said. "I had your determination too... Though perhaps not. You're serious aren't you?"

"Of course. I won't let them catch me, and if they do, I'll hurt them as badly as I can. We have to make this a better time, a better world. We can't let monsters rule us forever."

"You're talking about more than this village, aren't you?" Elly asked.

"Village?" Maia said. "I guess I shouldn't be surprised at all. They aren't travellers are they?"

"No," Elly said. "They've settled here. I don't know how long ago. But they found the place and moved in. Nothing to build, all in remarkably good condition. I think they may have murdered the previous occupants..."

"What a rotten bunch..."

"They really are. And none of them with the brains or the looks to suit as husbands. A bunch of tired, bitter old men out to get the best they can before they die. And at the expense of anybody who stands in their way."

"I'm sure the militia would be interested to learn of

them..."

"Which militia?" Elly asked. "Windsor doesn't normally come here. They stop at the turn at Wahroonga, and the city militia only come as far as the Lane Cove Tunnel. Any groups closer than that will become a target to this group eventually."

"Oh no," Maia gasped.

"What is it?"

"Wendy," she replied. "I wonder if she knows? That whole family is in danger."

"That depends," a familiar voice said in the darkness. "Not if we know about them and they don't know we know,"

"Wait," Maia said, combing her recent memory. "Nigel?"

"Indeed it is I, m'Lady," the man said with mock formality, approaching through the doorway from another room.

"But how?" Elly asked. "And who?"

"This is Nigel, he's from the place I stayed last night. He's a friend."

"I'm glad to hear that, young miss," Nigel said. "Wendy had heard some rumours of a secretive group operating in the area, so she asked me to follow you and ensure you were OK. It seems a good thing she did."

"Nigel, they took my horse, and all my things."

"Don't fret, Maia," he said, using her name for the first time since she met him. "I have a clear idea on where it all is. We'll get out of this building first, and you two will head straight for that gate. The cart, the lazy bastards left outside. Hide under it and wait for me there. I'll meet you with both horses. And I'll get all your possessions too. Don't worry, I'm a soldier at heart. I'll kill any that try to stop me."

"Maia," Elly whispered, casting a furtive glance at their rescuer, "Can we trust this most excellent man?"

"With our lives, Elly," Maia said, full of confidence. "We can trust this most excellent man with our lives and our honour."

Chapter 13 – Breakout

Alex walked beside the cart, his mother sitting on top, one horse, the sire of the colt Maia had taken, pulling the now empty cart on their journey home.

The sale of the colt had been intended to purchase supplies for the next season, but that was not to be. Furthermore, Alex's mother had graciously paid the bandits for Artemis, at Alex's insistence, in spite of funds being limited. The pup slept soundly on the cart, beside her as she drove.

The city militia had been uninterested in pursuing the matter of Maia, saying the words of one boy against a group of successful merchants was insufficient without evidence. Evidence being the alleged girl.

And so they now commenced the journey home, heading west out of the city to then turn south. Alex moped, not speaking after his mother insisted he return home with her. She looked down at her son now, as he walked in teenage surliness.

"I know you liked her, but we have work at home, and without the supplies, you'll be needed to help out to keep us going. We need to increase our own production of food, because we didn't bring anything back."

"I promised her. I said I'd find her."

"And still you might, but not just yet. Those men were dangerous, and you were reckless going with them."

"I couldn't give her back!"

"So you took her dog and you left her alone. With our horse. I know I said she could take it, but I had hoped you'd have the sense to see her to safety and bring the horse back."

"I had to give her the best chance to escape," Alex mumbled.

"And you did," she replied. "I'm proud of you for that, but you didn't leave her safe. She has a long way to go and a lot of trouble ahead. If I let you run after her, chances are you wouldn't ever find her, and you'd be just as dead as she might be come winter."

"So that's it? I go home and forget she ever existed?"

"That's not what I said, Son. We have a lot of work to do to keep ourselves fed. But if we can get that in place, perhaps then you can take your father, and the dog, and go after her. You'll be no help to her now, on your own, with those men out for blood."

Artemis woke, and wined, looking around. Alex's mother brought the cart to a halt.

"Lift the pup down, she'll be ready to go to the bathroom. She might enjoy a walk for a bit after that, now she is rested."

Alex fetched a rope, and secured it to the pup's collar before lifting her down. He walked the pup to the scraggly grass beside the road, where she immediately squatted.

"Good girl, Arty," Alex said, feeling the pup needed reassurance now she had lost her master.

Artemis soon finished, then walked back towards the cart, sitting at the end of the rope. The pup looked up at Alex, sadness in her eyes.

"I know, Arty," Alex said. "We'll find her one day, you'll just have to be patient. Come."

He started walking, and Artemis trotted along beside him, whining occasionally and looking around, far from the confident pup she had been with Maia.

"She does miss the girl," his mother said. "But we have to go about things the right way."

A group of men appeared over a low rise ahead, marching in military formation. They were in a quick step, and approached rapidly.

"Who's that?" Alex asked.

"It looks like a Militia. I don't know which town's though," his mother replied.

The men were in a basic militia uniform as worn by so many, a tan jerkin and pants, weapons holsters on belt and shoulder, the captain with a bright blue vest over the top. As they came close, one man darted from the rear of the group and rushed towards Alex.

"You there!" he shouted. "Boy, where did you get that dog?"

"Halt!" the captain shouted. "Civilian, you may not be a trained militia member, but protocol still applies. What is the meaning of this?"

"My apologies, Daryl, but that dog is Maia's. It's called Artemis, and it belongs to the girl who was taken.",

Daryl knelt down and looked at the dog, then at Alex.

"Drop the rope, boy."

Alex did as he was instructed, and Daryl held a hand out to the pup.

"Artemis, come."

The pup cautiously approached the soldier, sniffed his hand, and allowed the captain to pat her.

"It seems you are correct. The pup answers to its name. Boy, where did you get this animal?"

"It's Maia's. When the kidnappers caught up to us, I stalled them so she could escape, but they already caught Arty, so I returned in their custody while she got away, and my mother paid them for the dog so when I am able I can return it to her."

"Wait, when the kidnappers caught up?" Greg asked. "So you had escaped together?"

"Yes, one of the men in that band had tried to help, but with my mother's help Maia and I left the markets on our horse. Maia is still with the horse, but I don't know where she is now."

"What was that man's name?" Daryl asked. "We have some information, if you can confirm it, we can make life a little easier for that one when they are captured."

"Barry, I think," Alex replied.

"That was the name we were told in Blackheath," Greg said.

"Excellent," Daryl said. "Son, you have seen these men. Could you recognise them if you saw them again?"

"Yes," Alex replied.

"Excellent. Ma'am, your son must come with us."

"That is as well as it is, however he is needed at home. Our horse which was to sell to fund our supplies is now with the girl, so we are returning empty handed. We need him to help keep our settlement fed with his efforts."

"That will not be a problem. We can pay him as a consultant. Do you visit Windsor?"

"Not often, but once a year a trader comes from there to our home. They're due within the month."

"I will give you a promissory note. Buy whatever you require from the trader, give them the note, and the militia will pay. Any shortfall will be sent to you later. Will that be satisfactory?"

"Do you wish to go with them, Alex?" she asked.

"Of course," Alex replied. "I made a promise."

"Then it's agreed," she said. "I will take your note, and use it as you request. The trader may need to make a return trip, depending on what they have with them. That will cost extra."

"It will be covered," Daryl said, opening his pack and pulling out a note pad, envelope, and seal.

*　　　*　　　*

Maia and Elly remained in the apartment for a few hours, until dark. Nigel retreated to another room for a long while and Maia wondered if he had left. Eventually, the door opened and the woman entered, placed two plates of awful looking food on the table, then left without saying a word. Nigel walked in as the door closed.

"You don't have to eat that," Nigel said. "We don't know if they put anything in it to make you sleep or whatever, but regardless, it smells terrible. I wouldn't eat it. Wait here, I'll go scout the area. I think they'll be eating together, but we want you to escape without being seen."

He disappeared, and the girls heard a brief scuffle out the back, then silence. They waited several minutes after that eerie quiet began, and then he rushed into the room.

"OK, we have to hurry, before they find their man outside."

"What happened?" Maia asked.

"There was a guard outside the back door. He wasn't there earlier. He'll live, but he'll be a bit sore. If they find him before we leave, it will be bad."

"OK, Let's get out of here!" Elly said, a little too loud as she rushed past Nigel.

"Wait, there was a back door all this time?" Maia asked.

"It was locked and barricaded," Nigel said. I broke the lock coming in but staged the bar so it looked undisturbed. That guard got a surprise when I opened it from inside."

Exiting the building, Nigel led them around, and paused to scout ahead before waving them on. At the front door, they saw another man, unconscious, blood running from his temples.

"He doesn't muck around," Elly whispered to Maia. "You have useful friends."

They rushed down the path to the gate, and Nigel wrestled it open. Two guards lay sprawled on the ground outside, and Nigel dragged them back through the gate, stashing the bodies in the bushes beside the path.

"We can't have them waking up while you're out there with them," Nigel explained, ushering the girls through. "Quickly now, wait for me under the cart. I'll be back with your horses. Your belongings are in the cart already."

"How?" Elly muttered, and Nigel held his finger to his mouth, slipped through the gate, and pulled it closed.

The girls ran to the cart, Elly ducking under. Maia instead looked in the cart, found her saddle bag, and took out the old book before climbing under with Elly. The full moon lent some light, but not enough.

"What are you doing with that?" Elly asked.

"It's a book of maps. Those people know where I was planning to go. When they find us gone, where will they look?"

"So you want to find another way?"

"Yes, but Wendy warned me against going back the way I came. There has to be a third route to take."

"It's really too dark to see the map here," Elly complained. "You'll likely wind up following a river instead of a road."

"You're right. Maybe Nigel will know a way."

Taking a risk, Maia returned the book to the bag then rejoined Elly under the cart. They waited what felt an eternity, until the gate opened, and Nigel came out, leading two horses by ropes.

Once they were through, he turned them so he could reach back and pull the gate closed, then rushed to the cart. He connected the horses, then climbed on the front of the cart.

"Quickly now girls, they'll know what's happened soon, and we want to be far away. These two horses are not well matched for the cart, so we have to take it slow, but if they can trot for a bit, it will be a blessing."

The girls scrambled onto the cart and it rattled along the road, Nigel steering as best he could onto grass where it grew to try to reduce the noise.

"Nigel," Maia whispered as they passed the last of the wall surrounding the camp. "They know I was planning to go to Windsor. So they'll go looking that way. I don't want to go back. Do you know a third way to Windsor?"

"It's a long way, I mean a really long way, but you could go the old M1 motorway. That takes you the opposite direction, but then you can take the old roads back along the rivers to Wisemans Ferry, and find your way to Windsor from there."

"Are there any dangerous groups that way?"

"I don't know. There will be settlements, but take care. Remember how you didn't immediately trust Wendy at the hotel? That caution will serve you well."

"OK, so when there is more light, I'll consult the map book, and take the M1. Thanks, Nigel."

"My pleasure, girls," he said. "I'll get you to the M1, and then I'll have to leave you to it. Watch carefully how I drive the cart in the mean time. See how the horses respond to guidance? You're lucky both horses are trained, or this would have been a dog's breakfast."

"Dog's breakfast..." Maia whispered, sadness in her voice. "I miss Arty. I hope she's OK."

"That was your pup? I'm sure she'll be fine," Nigel said.

"You can't know that..."

"No, I can't, but from how you described him, you can have faith in that lad. Now then, you're taking the pacific motorway, not the pacific highway. I tell you this because it is easy to get confused. The motorway travels through a lot of areas without entering the settlements or the old towns. The highway you'd be passing a lot of settlements and your safety can't be guaranteed."

"I understand," Maia said. "I thought this was the Pacific highway we were already on?"

"It is. Like I said, these ancient roads can get confusing. Be sure to check your map book, so you know when to get off the motorway. And keep your eyes peeled for trouble. Try to run if you can, rather than confront it."

"Of course."

"Sorry to sound all motherly, but Wendy wouldn't forgive me if I let something happen, and I can't come with you."

The wide road wound like a serpent through the night, the moon casting a haunting glow to the abandoned streets. For a little under two hours, they travelled, the cart rattling over the weathered tarmac, every jostle bringing with it the fear of a pursuer discovering them.

Suddenly, Nigel caught the reins and pulled them to the right, as the road crossed a short bridge.

"I almost missed it," he said, pointing to a sign with the barely legible lettering "Newcastle M1," with an arrow pointing down a ramp to another, much larger road, which passed beneath the bridge.

Reaching the bottom of the ramp, the motorway spread ahead of them into the distance, tall trees and large amounts of bushes shrouding it in a protective screen against observers. The tarmac was cracked and broken, grasses and small shrubs slowly reclaiming the road for nature, but it was still passable for the cart and horses.

Nigel stopped, and climbed down from the cart, handing the reins to Maia. He paused, then turned to face them.

"I'm sorry but I must leave you here. I wish you both the best of luck. It's a long journey you have ahead. I'll watch the bridge for a while, if I see anyone following, I'll see to it they don't make it onto the motorway. But I have to return to the hotel, and report to Wendy. She'll be wanting to have that settlement taken care of. Goodbye, ladies."

With an uncharacteristic flourish of a bow, he ran back towards the ramp, leaving the girls to continue their way alone.

"What an interesting man he is," Elly said, smiling.

"He's certainly full of surprises," Maia said as she gave the reins a snap and the horses started walking again.

They travelled for another half hour and then some into the night, before Maia decided they needed proper rest, and so did the horses.

She steered the cart to the side of the road, where a small low banked area of scrub broke the endless wall alongside the motorway. There was a small blue sign nearby, with a strange symbol that resembled some kind of handle.

A box atop a post stood beside the sign, and the girls pondered it's meaning as they released the horses from the cart, then tethered them to a nearby railing, before climbing into the cart to sleep.

"I'll take first watch," Elly said. "I'll wake you in a few hours, if nothing happens before then."

"OK," Maia said, stifling a yawn.

Maia was asleep in moments, and Elly kept to her word, waking her as the moon dipped low in the sky. Maia then kept watch until the sky began to lighten with the promise of dawn. She woke her friend to help hitch up the horses, before allowing her to return to sleep as the cart rocked and bounced it's way north.

Chapter 14 – Brooklyn Bridge

Maia sat up front, while Elly slept in the cart through the early morning. It took some time to get used to the horses. She understood what Nigel meant when he said they were lucky both horses were trained, and that the horses were not well matched to pull the cart together.

In the rush to escape, he had tethered them to either side of the cart, outside a pair of arms that reached forward, with a leather breach at the rear to enable a steady descent. Maia had copied his tethering when she started in the morning.

Maia had been tired and it was dark when Nigel guided them down the ramp to the motorway, but now, as she tried to do the same on the descents as the motorway cut along the hilly landscape, Maia found it difficult.

Considering the issue, Maia recalled that Elly's kidnappers had only the one horse to pull the cart, so clearly the single animal was capable. Stopping the cart, she walked to the front and untethered the horse she had received from Alex.

Stroking its face gently, she complimented the horse with coos and whispers, as she guided it away from the front of the cart. She took the knotted rope and unravelled it into a longer tether, which she tied to a rail on the side of the cart.

Returning to the front of the cart, she untied the other horse, which allowed the two bars to swing back into their proper positions. Maia carefully guided the horse between the bars, but it was reluctant.

"It's name is Farrow," Elly said, having woken to the noise. "She'll respond better if you talk to her, and use her name. Doesn't your horse have a name?"

"I don't know, Alex never told me one."

"Well it has to have a name!" Elly said. "Surely you have some idea for him?"

"Honestly I hadn't even considered whether it was a him or a her," Maia said, embarrassed.

"Well it's clearly a him," Elly said with a laugh in her voice. "Is there any man who helped you that you might want to name him after?"

"I Could call him Uncle, but that would get confusing when I get home..."

"OK, So how about on your journey?"

"Well, I can't call him Alex, that will be weird if I see Alex again..."

"Nobody else?"

"Nigel?"

"Nigel is excellent, but his name doesn't suit a horse."

"Then..." Maia thought for a moment. "Barry? He was one of my abductors who tried to help me out. I think in a different situation, he would have seemed a nice man. He was trying to help without being seen to help, if you know what I mean."

"I guess the horse can be a Barry..."

"Well, I'll probably never see the man again, so it won't be awkward."

"Done, Barry the horse, thank you for all your help!"

"Barry and Farrow..."

"Or Farrow and Barry, they sort of work together..."

"The names do, and so do the animals. They tried so hard with the cart, even though they aren't well matched."

"Anyway," Elly said. "Let me help you with Farrow. I know she trusts me."

Elly jumped from the cart and walked to the front, where she took the rope from Maia's hand and stroked Farrow's face gently.

"Come on girl, back up, there you go," Elly said soothingly as the horse positioned itself between the bars.

"I think you're right, she trusts you more than me," Maia said.

"The harness goes like this," Elly said, quickly strapping Farrow into the complex set of ropes and straps which hung from the bars.

"It should be easier to control the cart now, because the breach will work properly for one horse, but it wasn't really designed for two."

"And I guess we can swap the horses if Farrow gets tired," Maia replied. "Wait, you actually know about this stuff?"

"Yeah, I used to rig the carts for my parents. This was my cart until that pack of lunatics caught me."

"So why am I driving?" Maia asked.

"You offered," Elly said as she climbed onto the cart. "I can drive if you'd prefer. But if you aren't tired, I wouldn't complain about some company."

"Alright then," Maia said, climbing on the cart and sitting beside Elly.

Elly got them moving and Farrow pulled the cart slowly along the motorway. Barry the horse stood there until the rope tugged, and he began to follow.

They travelled through the morning, marvelling at the landscape. Maia felt nervous as they passed through cuttings, where the ancient engineers had carved out entire hills, leaving immense rocky cliffs soaring upwards from either side of the motorway.

She knew those cliffs had stood for probably two centuries without falling, but the height still made her nervous as they towered overhead. And should a large enough group of bandits choose to attack, they could be trapped in between two groups with nowhere to go.

The road surface was badly weathered, but still a passable road. Elly kept the cart close to the centre island, where dense scrub had grown up to block the view of the other side.

"I hope there aren't any of these cutouts which have collapsed, we might not get through." Elly mused.

"We just have to hope," Maia replied. "We've been lucky so far."

"I hope our luck holds out."

They travelled without incident, not seeing any sign of people at all, until sometime soon after mid day, they stopped for a break. Farrow and Barry drank from their meagre supplies, and graised lazily on the edges of the motorway while Maia and Elly stretched their legs, then lay sprawled on the grass for a while. The horses were tethered with long ropes to an ancient guard rail.

The sky was darkening, and Maia awoke to a large drop of water splashing on her face. She didn't even realise she had fallen asleep, and she looked over to see Elly also sleeping, the horses milling around contentedly.

Maia looked at the sky, foreboding clouds blocking out the sun as more of the heavy rain drops splashed around them. She shook Elly awake, and together they fitted Barry to the harness and tethered Farrow to the rear of the cart, as a wicked wind began to whip at them, blasting rain drops into their faces.

"This is no good," Maia shouted, desperately trying to shield her face.

"We can't do much about it," Elly replied. "The weather is unpredictable and we always knew there were risks travelling. Get the spare tarpaulin from the cart, we can have some kind of shelter at least."

Maia climbed into the back and rummaged, finding a brown stiff fabric, identical to the one which lay in the floor of the cart. Thinking about it, she quickly stuffed all their possessions under the one on the floor, and opened out the spare.

Maia immediately regretted her actions as the wind whipped the fabric, and nearly ripped it from her hands, dragging her to the back of the cart. Pulling it low, she gathered it in over one arm, then slowly made her way back to the front, and climbed onto the bench next to Elly.

Taking care not to repeat her mistake, Maia slowly unfolded the fabric over their laps, then folded it around them, and over their heads, leaving a gap to see out of.

"It's a shame we can't do anything for the horses," Maia said.

"It is, but we'll just have to hope they're OK and push on."

"I've got an idea," Maia said, extracting herself from the tarpaulin and climbing into the back again.

Rummaging, she found the old book and stuffed it under her clothing before climbing back up the front and wriggling back inside the protecting fabric.

"Perhaps the maps can show us a place to shelter."

"I doubt it, but it's worth a look," Elly replied.

Maia took out the book, and holding it within the tarpaulin she strained her eyes, trying to see in the diminished light. She soon found the page where they had last been, and tried to follow the line of the motorway north.

"I think you're right," Maia moaned. "I can't really see, but all the lines and things don't tell me much without proper light."

"Have you seen the bridges which go over head?" Elly asked.

"Yeah, They'll be other old roads which they wanted to not join the motorway. I'm not sure why."

"Can you see the lines for those roads?"

"Yeah, the next one is a long way away. We'll probably be ready to stop for the day by the time we get there. It's a short distance before a place called Brooklyn, we might want to get off the motorway and find an old house or something to sleep in there."

"We'll just have to push on then, but if I find a place to stop, we can at least wait out the rain for a while."

They continued, progress slow, as the darkness only deepened. Soon, they were unable to see the sides of the motorway, and they couldn't even tell if the road was turning until they came up against the island in the middle, which resembled a lower version of the walls on either side.

Elly kept the cart close to that island, and followed it's line as best she could. Farrow was becoming distressed, but still pushed on. Barry pulled the cart regardless, his fortitude one small grace in a terrible day. Maia worried, and wondered if they'd survive to see the evening.

Finally, late in the afternoon, the clouds parted, and a bright sun cast sharp, long shadows across the motorway. Elly took the opportunity as the rain subsided to check over the horses and the cart. Satisfied, they continued.

Finally, they found themselves on a long descent, and Maia consulted the book, barely able to make out the lines in the shadow of the motorway cliffs.

"It looks like we're coming up to Brooklyn, but I can't

see how we get down there from the motorway."

"We just have to go until we see something I guess," Elly replied.

The trees and rocks to the right began to clear, and in the distance, they could see water, with more hills beyond.

"That's a river," Maia said, looking at the book again. "A big one. We'll be crossing it soon."

"I still haven't seen anywhere to get off the motorway. We must have missed it already."

"Don't worry, we'll find something. I just hope that rain doesn't come back."

As the sky grew dark and a bright moon lit the road, they found themselves passing onto a long, flat bridge over an immense body of water. A second bridge to the right, with rusted steel arches, ran parallel to the one they were on.

"So much for Brooklyn. We'll see what's on the other side," Maia said.

The bridge seemed to go on and on, but finally to the left the land reached up to meat them, and they could see in the moonlight a large flat area with grass and trees. There was a break in a guardrail, and Elly steered the cart through. They made their way into the stand of trees.

"Who goes there?" shouted a woman, stepping out of the trees, brandishing a flaming torch.

"Just travellers, passing through," Elly shouted back.

"A girl?" the woman said, approaching them and holding the torch up to better see the pair on the cart. "It's a wicked road to be travelling alone, ladies,"

"It's a wicked time all around," Maia replied. "That storm was awful."

"Indeed it was, you two must be soaked to the skin! Come now, I live alone here, but I do have shelter and a fire. It's a good thing too, you might have gone to Brooklyn and then you'd be in trouble."

"Trouble?" Maia gasped. "Why? We had thought of stopping there when I saw it on the map, but we missed the way off the motorway."

"Just as well you did, child," the woman replied. "There is a sickness in Brooklyn these days. For the good of the rest of the settlements, once you go in, they don't let you back out."

"What kind of sickness?" Elly asked.

"One of those viruses from the old times, they say. People get sick, and eventually they stop breathing. I'm not aware of the finer details, you understand, but I have no intention of going there to find out for myself."

"I wonder how they got it?" Maia wondered.

"It doesn't matter," the woman said. "The point is, they have it, and they intend to contain it. The mayor of that village is a smart man. He's old now, but he remembers well the tales of his grandparents. A traveller brought the illness to them, but he's determined not to let one take it elsewhere."

"How do you know then?" Elly asked.

"My son is there. He sent a pigeon with news about a month ago. He said in a week, fifty of their people had died. The mayor has said until there are no deaths for a six-month, the town will be closed. Come now, that's enough talk of misery. Let's get your horses watered and you two inside."

""I'm Maia, by the way, and this is Elly."

"Oh how rude of me!" the woman exclaimed. "My name is Fran. My home isn't much, but it's shelter. Come."

Climbing from the cart, the girls, too tired to argue the point with their benefactor, untied the horses and led them after the women, where she showed them to a trough full of rain water, inside a fenced yard. They released the horses there and Fran shut the gate once the girls were back outside the yard.

"I don't have horses, very few people do. But sometimes travellers need a place to stay, and they do sometimes have animals. Usually they have a proper carriage, but I can't let you two sleep in the open. You'll catch a chill after coming through that rain."

Out of the darkness, under the shade of the trees, they approached a large circular tent. Fran pulled aside a flap and ushered them inside. It was warm, a fire near the centre sending smoke out through a flue, which was attached via steel supports to the centre post of the tent.

The flue ended beneath a small fly which stopped the rain from getting in, the smoke billowing around it to vanish into the night.

It was a sparse and simply furnished home, but it seemed comfortable to the girls after their long day. The fire kept the spacious tent warm, and many blankets were hung around the walls, providing extra insulation from the weather outside. They stood near the entry for a moment while Fran went and placed a pot of water on a stand over the edge of the fire, and added some kindling beneath it.

"There are blankets in the basket beside the door, you two should get out of those wet clothes and dry off. Just lay your clothes out anywhere, they'll dry soon enough."

The girls did as they were told, soon wrapped in warm woollen blankets and seated on small wooden stools before the fire.

"These blankets are so luxurious," Maia mused. "Fran, your home might be just a tent, but there is much wealth in your possessions. Thank you for sharing your home with us."

"It's my pleasure. As I said, I usually don't take visitors into the house, but in your cases, I'm willing to make an exception. Here you go."

Fran poured the hot water into cups, into which she dropped steel infusers filled with some kind of dried leaves. She handed a cup to each girl and took one herself, sipping it slowly.

"What is this?" Elly asked, nervously tasting the hot beverage.

"It's a tea made from local grasses," Fran said, taking a long sip from her own cup. "Don't worry, it's perfectly safe. It will warm you right up."

Fran fetched a third stool and sat to the side of the fire, facing the girls.

"Now tell me, what on earth could lead two pretty young girls like you to be travelling through a place like this?"

"We were both kidnapped." Elly said.

"In different places, at different times, by different people," Maia explained. "But yes, we were both taken against our will, have escaped, and now are trying to get home."

"I'm not," Elly said. "I really don't have a home anymore. I was on my own when I was taken, because I left the village when it was attacked. So I'm following Maia, I'll go to her home."

"And where is that?" Fran asked.

"Well, I'm from a village in the mountains, but if I can get to Windsor, I will make my way from there."

"Windsor? You're travelling the wrong way, girls."

"We know," Maia replied. "But Elly's kidnappers know that was where I was going, and have control of the roads we'd have normally taken."

"I see," Fran said, thinking for a moment before continuing. "You're trying to get to Wisemans Ferry, and go the really long way around. But how did you know about that route?"

"I found a book, an ancient book of maps. I learned of it that way."

"I see, so you are a resourceful young lady then. Good, you'll need that. But I can offer you some advice. Don't just rely on the maps. A lot of things have changed, and the most important thing is the people. If you follow the maps you might miss the good ones and meet the bad."

'I've seen enough now that I can well believe you," Maia said. "But we've been fortunate so far."

"Good fortune will only take you so far. But tell me your story, and I'll see what advice I can give."

And so Maia recounted the long tale of her journey. Her abduction, Barry's help, meeting Alex and escaping with him, losing Alex and Artemis, finding Elly and Nigel helping, everything she could remember in a long and rambling tale.

And when she was done, Fran smiled.

"There is somewhere you should go, before Wisemans Ferry, and if you follow your maps, you will never go there. Instead of leaving the motorway, you should stay on it. It's only another hour by foot from the turn off, and you'll meet some friends of mine. They can help you in ways far more important than simply getting you home.

But now, you should sleep. We'll talk again in the morning."

Chapter 15 – Mooney Creek

Maia woke at dawn, to find Fran not in the tent. Rising, she added some wood to the fire, dressed, and left Elly snoring softly in her blankets. Walking into the morning light, the place was much prettier than it had been the night before.

Maia walked through the trees and found Barry and Farrow in the pen, contentedly nibbling at the grass. When they saw Maia, they wandered over to the gate, and she smiled as she stroked their necks.

"You two look fine today. I'm glad."

Following the fence, she made her way around and out into the open grassed area. The grasses brushed against her legs as she walked. They grew all the way to the river's edge, where she could see Fran, seated on a rock, fishing line in hand.

Maia walked to the woman and remained quiet, watching as Fran wrestled a bream out of the water and dropped it into a wooden bucket, then cast again. Maia sat on a rock and watched for several minutes, until Fran had pulled in another fish, dropped it in the bucket, and stood.

"Good Morning, Maia," Fran said, her voice cheerful. "I've got the three of us a fish each. The Hawkesbury still provides me plenty, and it's so beautiful to sit and watch."

"The Hawkesbury?"

"The river," Fran explained. "It's called the Hawkesbury River. Travellers tell me it's one of the most beautiful rivers in the world, and I get to live along side it."

"It is beautiful here. I'm surprised you haven't got lots of other people wanting to live here."

"They tend to settle in Brooklyn. Settlers want access to shops, to carpenters, to builders, to blacksmiths, to all the comforts and company a village can provide. They see this place, then they see Brooklyn, and they always settle there. That's fine by me. I'm happy for visitors, but I don't want neighbours."

"You direct them to Brooklyn, don't you?" Maia said, with a laugh in her voice as they began walking back towards the tent.

"But of course. They stop here, marvel at how pleasant it is, then they want something. It might be a question of fresh produce, a fixed wheel for their carts, horse shoes, it could be anything. And even if I can provide it to them, I send them to Brooklyn. Not at the moment of course, because of the illness, but thankfully since that began you two girls are the only travellers to come here. When they see Brooklyn, an established little town with empty homes to be taken, with all the same scenery I have plus a tavern, the boating facilities, they see a paradise, and I get to keep mine."

"Is it far? We missed the way down from the motorway."

"There are a couple of ways. If you're walking, you take the old railway bridge instead. On the motorway, you have two choices. There's an exit to an older, more hazardous bridge near where you left the road to find me, or you have a long way back to the exit you missed onto a winding road down to the town. It's long, but a beautiful scenic trip. Or otherwise, normally every couple of days my son brings a barge up the river. He brings supplies to me here, and takes stuff to and from several other settlements along the river. Most travellers are happy to use his barge to get their things to Brooklyn, even if they walk to go there at first and come back for their things later."

"What would you do now? With Brooklyn closed?"

They stopped by a large wooden block, and Fran set about gutting the fish as they talked.

"I'd direct them over the other side of the motorway. There are old houses there. All along the river edge, big old homes that rich people must have built. They're empty now, but the people who choose to live in them could take a boat to Brooklyn if they had one, or walk the railway bridge and be there in an hour. And they don't need to build anything."

"So you get to keep your paradise and the abandoned houses get resettled. Good thinking."

"I think so. If I was interested in such a house, it's where I'd go. But I like my simple life here."

"I'd like to visit you again someday, for more than a night, if that would be OK?"

"Of course, I'd be glad of the visit. You two girls are welcome any time. But don't go getting ideas of settling on my patch."

"I wouldn't dream of it! The solitude is so much of the beauty of the place."

"I'm glad you understand. Of course, if you wanted a bit of solitude like this for yourself, there is a lovely stretch of shore line west of here, as well as an island. Peat island has some people on it, but there is more than enough room for another settler or two."

Leaving the fishing line and bucket, Fran took the three gutted and filleted fish and continued towards the tent, Maia following. Elly stood in the tent entry, rubbing her eyes as they approached.

"Elly, can you take the pot and fetch some water from the river for me? Maia, get your map while I cook breakfast. We'll look over your travel plans for today."

"OK," Maia said, heading for the cart where their belongings had been left the night before.

"OK," Elly said, yawning as she went into the tent, coming back out with a pot and walking towards the river.

Maia watched her friend, thinking about how pleasant this place would be to live, if only they could. With Elly saying last night she had no home to go back to, Maia felt a pang of guilt that she was dragging the girl into the mountains instead of giving her somewhere as perfect as this.

"I guess it's Elly's choice," Maia mumbled. "If she hates it in Gospers, she can come back down here later."

Fetching the book, Maia returned to the tent and entered just as Elly was returning with the water. The smell of fresh fish frying over the flames assailed her, and it was beautiful.

"I hope that fish tastes as good as it smells," Maia said.

"Nothing tastes better than fresh fish from a clean river," Fran replied, pointing at a wooden cupboard. "If you look in the pantry you'll find some bread and a wrapped butter. Can you cut us a thick slice of bread each to toast?"

Maia went to the pantry and found the bread and butter, then placed them on the table where Fran had left a bread knife already. Carefully, she cut three slices and carried them to the fire.

Fran handed her an implement consisting of two wire grills hinged together with a long handle. Maia placed the bread between the grills and held it in the flames, turning it over every few seconds until the bread was golden.

Taking it back to the table, she found three plates stacked at one end, and put a hot slice on each, then took the grills and hung them from a hook near the fire, where Fran pointed.

By the time Maia had buttered the three slices of toast, Fran had finished with the fish and carried them over in the pan. Fran slipped a fish onto each plate, next to the toast, then returned to the fire, where the water was starting to boil.

More tea, like they had last night, was soon prepared, and they sat around the table to eat. The fish was beautifully flavoured, and the toast and butter simple but satisfying. Once they were finished eating and all sipping tea, Fran looked at Maia.

"Now then, show me that map."

Maia opened the book to their current location and passed it across the table. Fran raised an eyebrow as she took it and looked at the page Maia had opened it to.

"This is a rare find," Fran said. "These old books are difficult to come by, and very useful, even if many roads are gone."

"It's served me well so far," Maia replied.

Fran ran a finger up the page, then turned over, continuing to follow the motorway across pages.

"OK, so you would have been headed to this exit, to

Peats Ridge Road. I suggest you go beyond that, and follow the motorway as it turns east. What you'll find is a large settlement on, and inside of, a massive bridge. They have power. I mean electricity, not might. They have knowledge. They have built a good life for themselves there, and can offer you a lot of good advice to improve your village when you get home."

"On and inside of?" Elly asked.

"My friend Graham, well, I say friend, he's my son's father, he lives there. He says it was called a twin cantilever bridge. It's structure is hollow, and has enough space inside the span to shelter a good sized village. And it spans a huge gully, with strong winds. They've lined the span with wind turbines, so they have all the lighting and heating and other comforts they could need. They trade a lot with Brooklyn, and with other settlements further north."

"They have electricity? Throughout the village?" Maia asked.

"Yes, and all the old things, those that still work. They live a life far more advanced technologically than many in this world today. If anybody can help you help your village, it's them. They will be valuable trading partners."

"I see," Maia said. "Then we will pay them a visit, before heading to Wisemans Ferry."

"Please do. And tell them about Brooklyn, so they stop sending traders for a while. They need their traders to return home, and if they send them to Brooklyn, they won't get back out."

"We will," Maia said, standing. "Thank you Fran, for everything. But we should get going. How long will it take to reach the bridge?"

"Between five and six hours," Fran replied. "But take care, I'd hate it if something bad happened to you two."

"We'll be careful," Elly said. "Thanks."

Taking the book, Maia and Elly left the tent, retrieved the horses, and started to hitch Farrow to the cart. Fran followed them out, and stopped them with a hand on the horse's rump.

"Wait, the other horse is better suited to the first

section. You have a steep hill to climb, you don't want to exhaust this poor mare in the first hour of the day."

Taking her advice, the girls hitched Barry to the cart, and tethered Farrow to the back. Fran gave them a barrel of water, a sack of feed grass for the horses, and a bucket, which they gladly accepted. Smiling, and waving, they bid fond farewell to Fran and the cart rattled back onto the motorway, to continue the journey north.

Just as Fran had said, they soon found themselves travelling up a long incline, but the gradient was not beyond the abilities of Barry, and while slow, they made steady progress as the motorway wound its way up hill.

The scenery mirrored what they had passed through the day before, with the happy exception of the weather. The sun remained this time, and the wind stayed gentle. Maia and Elly were glad to be dry, and the warmth of the sun was a pleasant sensation as they rode in the cart.

By late morning, as they passed beneath a bridge on which somebody had painted "Morgan's Road," Barry was slowing. They stopped in the shade of the bridge, and watered the horses, before swapping Farrow to the front, so Barry could have a rest from pulling the cart.

They gave the horses some of the feed from the sack, before sitting to eat some jerky which still remained in Maia's pack from Wendy.

Refreshed, they continued on their way, in far better spirits than the same time the day before. Maia took out the book, and stared at the maps for a while.

"It looks like we're about halfway to Peats Ridge Road, which we are going to pass instead of taking, if we want to visit that bridge Fran told us about."

"And she said that was about an hour further, right?" Elly said. "Then we have plenty of time, we should get there well before dark."

"Yeah, that's what I think too," Maia said. "Unless something bad happens..."

"We've been lucky so far," Elly said.

"Not as lucky as you might think," Maia reminded her. "I lost Alex and Artemis, we both got taken by those people in that walled settlement, we had the horrible rain yesterday..."

"But we met each other, you met that Wendy person and her family, we met Fran yesterday, we didn't get stuck in Brooklyn, I'd say all things considered, we're doing pretty well."

"I hope it keeps going well then," Maia said. "You're right. If I hadn't been taken by those people, I wouldn't have met you, we wouldn't be travelling with the cart, I'd likely be facing some other horrible trouble back on the other road to Windsor. Everything seems to be happening in the way it has to. There must be a reason."

"Don't go sounding religious on me, Maia!" Elly said. "Just trust us to get us where we need to go. We'll make it, you watch us."

"Yeah, we will. I wonder what these bridge people are like?"

"I'm sure they're good people. I don't think Fran would send us there otherwise."

They continued on their journey, passed the Peats Ridge Road exit, and followed the motorway as it turned east. It was late afternoon when finally the enormous bridge came into view at the bottom of a long downhill stretch. They could see from a long way away that the bridge had a lot of things built on it, and many wind turbines span slowly in the wind.

A barricade blocked the road at the end nearest them. From a distance, the girls could see there were many animals in pens, though they couldn't quite tell what they were. Two horse riders started up hill to meet them.

"I really hope these people are friendly," Maia muttered as Elly continued to drive the cart down the road towards the approaching riders.

Before long, two young men sat before them, their horses smaller and faster than Barry and Farrow. The men looked at the girls with suspicion at first, then as they took in the scene, and rode around the cart to see there was nobody else, seemed to calm a little.

"What brings you this way?" one of the men asked.

"A lady named Fran suggested we come here. We were going towards Wisemans Ferry, but she suggested we visit your settlement first. She says you may be able to offer us advice or help."

"You should speak to the village elders," the other man said. "Follow us. We will store your cart and stable your horses while you go inside."

Chapter 16 – In The Bridge

As they approached the bridge, it's size was daunting, even from the road above the structure. A man and a woman dragged open the gate and they passed through. It was a massive, wooden contraption, with salvaged wheels from ancient vehicles to allow it to move.

The wheels were missing the rubber tires, instead wrapped with twisted fabric in a futile attempt to make them turn easily without scraping on the road.

As they passed through, the girls climbed down off the cart, and the gates closed behind them. The woman at the gate whispered something to the men, and then walked away.

"Follow Miriam, she will take you to the village," the man who had first greeted them said. "We will store your possessions here, and your horses will be refreshed when you leave."

Maia and Elly were nervous as they followed the woman, who did not speak as she led them across the bridge. It was a long way, the bridge spanning a wide gorge, it's height and length both amazing to Maia.

"This bridge is incredible," Maia said. "From up here, I can't see what kind of bridge it is, but it must be strong.'

As they walked, they passed pens in which dozens upon dozens of pigs were housed, and along the centre of the bridge, between it's two directions of travel, stood a long line of sturdy poles, atop which wind turbines span in the steady breeze that blew through the gorge.

There were many people working in the pig sty, as well as others who cultivated herbs and vegetables in immense concrete pots. They looked up with curious eyes as the girls passed, but none of them spoke.

Maia paused, to gaze between two shacks and out along the gorge, to the west. The scale of the place was incredible. This was the antithesis of the city, with it's endless concrete and buildings. Now, there was nothing but forest, lining the walls of the gorge all the way to the river below.

The sun was low, it's brightness blinding as she looked, a haze from the eucalyptus forest forming a precursor to the sunset. Maia felt a tug on her arm. Tearing her eyes away from the scenery, she found Miriam, impatiently dragging her away.

As they reached the northern end of the bridge, another set of gates blocked the way, however they were further off the bridge. Miriam led them close, then turned to the left, and followed an ancient, crumbling concrete path with a rusted steel hand rail around and down beside the bridge.

Then they found a set of much more recent stone stairs, which led to a platform, where a ladder led to a hatch. Miriam knocked on the hatch, and it was opened from the inside. In the shade under the bridge, the artificial light from inside was surreal, and Maia hesitated.

Miriam dragged at her arm, and pointed at the hatch. Elly rushed up the ladder and inside, and feeling no point in resisting, Maia followed, with Miriam behind.

'Halt, strangers!" ordered a man as they stood there, letting their eyes adjust to the sudden brightness. "What is your business?"

"A woman called Fran suggested your village could be of assistance." Elly said.

"Fran? What is that troublesome woman up to now?" the man muttered. "Fine, Miriam, take them to the elders."

As Miriam led them away from the hatch Maia and Elly took in their strange new surroundings. Inside the bridge was a giant cavern, with the floor sloping down and away. The walls were lined with bright electric lights. Curtains and partitions separated out areas for the residents to live.

As the floor grew steeper, wooden boards were erected, and stepped down, to provide flat surfaces. Judging the distance, Maia felt the cavern, while huge, was not the full width of the bridge. There must have been multiple such areas.

She was still wondering about the structure when Miriam pulled aside a curtain and ushered them into a small room. Three people sat there, awaiting their arrival.

"The gate keepers have sent word of your visit," an elderly woman said. "Please, ladies, take a seat. That will be all, Miriam."

Miriam bowed low, then scurried out of the room as if terrified.

"Please excuse Miriam. We do not know what made her the way she is, but we offer her sanctuary for as long as she needs."

"She's not from here?" Maia asked.

"Not originally. She came wandering up from the river nearly ten years ago, wounds across her back, climbing with a broken leg, a gash across her forehead. Something horrific is buried in that woman's memory, but she barely speaks. She has language, and she has intelligence, and she is a hard worker, but sadly we are not equipped to give her the psychological help she requires."

'That poor woman," Elly murmured.

"Indeed," one of the others, a man with a shaggy grey mop of hair said. "It is a dangerous world out there, so for two young ones like yourselves to arrive, safe and unharmed, with a cart and horses, you have piqued our interest. And to have you sent by Fran, there must be a mutual benefit to be had."

"Mutual?" Maia said. "I'm not sure what we can give you, or what you can give us. I see you have electricity, you are clearly well established with your piggery and vegetable farming operations on the span above."

"Perhaps if you tell us your story," the woman said, "we will understand why Fran thought to send you to us."

Maia spared no detail, explaining her journey so far just as she had done to Fran. In the process, she remembered the message about Brooklyn.

"Brooklyn is closed, because of an illness. Nobody who goes there is permitted to leave, as they fear the illness being spread to other communities."

"Then it is indeed fortunate you arrived to tell us of this," the third elder, a man in his late fifties, said. "We have a trade envoy preparing to leave for Brooklyn in the coming days. But trade does give me another notion, if my fellow elders will indulge me to speak of it?"

"Go ahead, Hugh," the woman said before addressing Maia. "Hugh is the youngest of we elders, and has spent his life in service of trade, so he knows the settlements and trade routes of this world rather well."

"Young lady, you speak of a village called Gospers. I have heard tell of this place. Like our own settlement, it was built after the end of the old times, if I am not mistaken?"

"That's true," Maia replied. "Our village was settled by those fleeing the larger towns and cities to escape from the various troubles."

"I had wondered about your village. We have heard of you through the traders who go to Windsor. You produce poultry goods, am I correct?"

"Yes, we do."

"And your white dogs are well known among traders, as they are an unusual method of haulage. I doubt the men who took your pup would find her easy to sell, regardless of their story because of that."

"I hope that isn't bad for her..."

"Indeed, but no, I dare say they will sell her to your young friend rather than not sell her at all."

"I hope so, he will look after her."

"Now, this is the first time our two settlements have met in person. You are here having left your village as a trader, and while your route to us is circuitous and not at all trade related, does that situation place you in a position to act on behalf of Gospers for the purpose of trade?"

"I guess it does," Maia replied.

"I would expect the same," Hugh continued. "Your poultry products, which I have sampled via other traders who have offered them in markets further afield having obtained them from Windsor, are of excellent quality. Geographically, we are not distant from each other, however the terrain is unforgiving, which has resulted in our long separation. I propose that separation be brought to an end."

"To an end?" Maia asked. "You mean, establish trade relations between the bridge and Gospers?"

"Yes, that is correct," Hugh replied. "We refer to ourselves as Mooney Bridge in these times, as it is simpler than explaining the old names in full. I am sure you understand that, being from a settlement on Gospers Mountain."

"Yes, I do," Maia replied. "But as you have said, the terrain is unforgiving. How would we establish trade relations?"

"As I have said, we have traded in the past with Windsor. Our primary trade routes from Mooney Bridge are north to the Gosford-Wyong areas where there is a trade post established for the various settlements in the area at the old Ourimbah interchange, and into the old city where you have been. However we also travel for trade to Windsor some years, and also into an area previously known as the North Shore, where a cluster of settlements trade in a place known as Narrabeen, on the site of what was once a holiday park. I believe it was called Sydney Lakeside Holiday Park in the old times."

"That's a wide area,' Maia said. "An impressive trade empire."

"Not as impressive as it may sound to you. It merely takes advantage of our location and the old road networks to travel equal distances in various directions. We have not traded into Gospers before now because there was no need. However, I feel your produce would be advantageous to us, and ours to you. We could provide your village with a steady supply of pork products, to offer greater dietary variety to both."

"Then how do we establish such a trade route?" Maia asked.

"To begin with, it may be beneficial to agree to meet in a third location, Windsor for example. But that is not ideal. We would be required to pay commissions and tariffs for all trades to Windsor, which is OK when trading there and benefiting from their protection, but in the longer term, a direct route will be advantageous. It will halve the time of travel for traders, and reduce the expenses incurred."

"And how would we establish such a route?'

"We need to build a road," Hugh said. "It will be the first such construction project in a century, and will take much effort. However if done the right way, it can bring our settlements together in mutual benefit."

"I am in agreement," Maia said. "As I look around your settlement, I see a lot of advantage for the people of Gospers. You have electricity. Outside of my mentor's home, we do not. I do have some understanding of how it works, and may be able with the right artefacts to get something working, but you have the experience and the expertise we may wish to borrow for such infrastructure improvements."

"And in Gospers with your mentor," the woman said, "It does sound like you have access to a cultural library we lack in Mooney Bridge. Our founders had knowledge and technical expertise to pass on, but not that heritage of history which defines a people in more um, spiritual or cultural terms."

"I have music in my belongings, on old discs, and a computing device which can play it, if you are interested in hearing it."

"Young lady," the older of the two men said. "It would be our honour if that treasure were shared with us. We of the bridge have the electricity to power our lights, our heating, and our cooking equipment. But the use of that power for entertainment is little more than a lost dream for most of us here. It shames me to admit, that with the luxury of peace and plenty, we have still not had the ability to avail ourselves of such things. And yet you, with your mentor and his vision, have kept so much of the old world alive. It may not be food, but your cultural wealth is immense, and if you will share it with us, we will ensure you are recompensed handsomely."

"However we are getting ahead of ourselves," the woman said. "The first order of business should be to locate a map. We have maps showing the roads which we travel for trade. We will require something much more detailed, preferably showing in detail the terrain of the mountains, but even if it does not, something with the old fire trails through the forests and the roads nearby would be of immense value in planning the route to be built."

"I," Maia said slowly. "May have something that will help. In my possessions I have an ancient book of maps. I used it to find my way out of the city, as I already mentioned. Those maps may provide the clues we seek."

"Then I ask you retrieve that book," the woman said. "And your music devices, and return here. We will commence our planning, and listen to the sounds of old."

Maia retrieved the items, and they poured over the maps for hours, debating the meanings and the directions, until they had agreed on a likely route. They would go back to Peats Ridge Road, and follow the route to Wisemans Ferry for a while, then cut across the mountains using old trails as much as possible from the place marked on the maps as Mangrove Mountain.

The elders would send a scout to explore that way, their goal to see how far they can travel and assess the roads for clearing. On her return to Gospers, Maia would arrange for an expedition from that end, hoping to meet at a place called Hopwoods Lagoon.

The fire trails and old roads should make it easier, and it would become a shorter trade route than going via Windsor, but much work still lay ahead.

They stopped for a late meal, and then took the discs and the device to the entry, where they connected it to power and entertained the bridge people long into the evening with the haunting voices of those long dead.

Chapter 17 – Gift of Power

Maia woke early, and made her way outside, before walking around the trail and onto the span of the bridge. The place was already bustling in the dawn light, with people moving around to tend to the animals and harvest vegetables for the days meals.

She made her way along the span, until she reached the place at the far end where the cart had been stored. In a stable nearby, she found Barry and Farrow, and bid them both a fond hello. While she was there, Hugh approached.

"Maia, I believe I can be of further assistance to Gospers."

She looked at him as she turned away from Barry, who nudged her, resenting the conclusion of the attention she had been giving.

"How do you mean?' she asked.

"You said Gospers only has electricity at one home, that of your mentor."

"That's correct."

"I know of a place, long abandoned, and separate from any settlement, which still lights up each evening with power collected from the sun. I believe we can help you retrieve those panels and lights, to be taken to Gospers. Additional cabling we can trade from our stores."

"That sounds wonderful, but why did you not harvest that equipment for yourselves?"

"We haven't needed them. The effort required in transporting them was greater than the trades available as those in need have long ago salvaged from somewhere nearer to themselves. Our location provided wind all year around, so we left the equipment where we found it. Gospers will be better served by solar power, so this may be a good opportunity to obtain it."

"How do we get it?" Maia asked.

"You have a cart, it should be able to carry a good

amount of equipment. You won't require all that is there, but I will accompany you, with some of our more technically minded young people, and assist in gathering enough to make some improvements to life on the mountain."

Maia agreed, this was a good idea. She went to find Elly, while Hugh had the stable hands move the horses and the cart to the northern end of the bridge, where they hitched Barry to the cart.

Maia returned with Elly, just as Hugh arrived with three other men, carrying large bags of tools and equipment, and they set out. The sun was warm, and the road was clear, so they made good time.

The men walked or jogged along side the cart as they travelled. It was almost an hour later, as they made their way up a slight incline, that Maia noticed something unusual. The bush land to the west of the motorway had clearly been burned some time in the last few years.

The trees were thinned out by intense fire, but the landscape was vibrant and green with new growth. In the middle distance, perched near the top of a rise, stood an enormous creature. It was grey, weathered concrete, an artefact from the old times.

"Is that…?" Maia asked.

"Yes, it's a dinosaur. A diplodocus, I believe it's the actual size the creatures were in ancient times. The statue marked the location of a zoo, or a park, of some kind."

They continued a short distance, then Hugh pointed at an exit from the motorway.

"We need to go that way, and follow it around and cross the motorway. The place we're going is a little way along that road."

Elly, holding the reigns, steered the cart as he had told them, and they left the motorway. Two lanes of road left the motorway to pass through a cutting, steep stone walls on either side. After a sweeping curve, they passed beneath the motorway out into the open, trees thick on either side.

"So the fires didn't cross the motorway?" Maia asked.

"They have done, many times," Hugh replied. "but the most recent ones two seasons ago were halted by an unseasonable storm."

They continued, and soon their two lanes were joined by two more, which curved away back towards the motorway to join it on the side opposite where they had left it. Now the four lanes, joined as a single larger road, met another from the left at a wide intersection. Battered lights hung out over the roads.

Hugh pointed to the far side of the intersection, on the left.

"Beyond those trees, that's our destination. We turn in at the next intersection."

The signs for the place were badly weathered and illegible, but there was a symbol Maia could see which was a circle with something resembling an L in it. Through the trees, she could see a selection of buildings, separated by large, open spaces.

They continued further, until they reached another intersection, at the far end of the peculiar complex. At that end, there was another sign, a circle divided into four quarters, two coloured white and two blue.

As Elly turned the cart into the complex, Maia looked at it, and felt it seemed familiar. A lot like somewhere she had been before. Then as she saw a line of ancient vehicles, she realised. And she felt the tears welling up as she gasped.

"No, not a place like this," She moaned.

"What is it? What's wrong?" Hugh asked.

"I found another place like this. I went looking at the old vehicles. In one of them I found a dead child, probably less than two when it died. It shook me up a little."

"Yes, I suppose that would shake anybody," Hugh said. "Even if the child died a century ago. It was like that for many people in those times. The things which killed them would strike without warning. It may be they were coming for the child, and died before they could return, or it could be the child died and they couldn't handle the burial. I pray we never see such times."

"But why a place like this?" Maia asked.

"These places sell the vehicles, it could be they intended to replace their vehicle, and were killed while selecting a new one. We wouldn't be able to tell now, but perhaps their vehicle had a fault, or was just too old to be safe. Or perhaps the place you saw was just a parking lot, not a place to sell the vehicles but a place to leave them while performing errands."

"It had similar signs to these, and a building at one side, so I think it was similar to this place."

"What do you suppose killed those people?" Elly asked.

"One of the many viruses," Hugh said. "Or perhaps they were involved in an environmental event, like a big fire or lightning storm, or perhaps they were killed by other people, desperate for supplies or money. It could even have been an escaped animal from one of the zoos, if it was later in the collapse. We'll never know. Those times had so many dangers, we are lucky people survived at all."

"Could a virus have killed them so quickly?" Maia asked.

"It may have, or if it had rapid onset of symptoms, they may have chosen to leave the child rather than infect it, hoping to find somebody they could send to fetch it. There were a lot of hard choices back then, based on the things we know."

"You seem to know a lot," Maia said. "I thought the elders said you had limited knowledge beyond survival. Our arts and the like were valuable for that reason."

"This is true, but I am fortunate. Unlike most of my people, I have travelled widely as a trade envoy. I have had to learn much of this land's history in order to understand the people I negotiated with. This knowledge is why I was permitted to become an elder of the bridge while still so young."

"Sorry to interrupt, but where are we heading?" Elly asked.

"Just pull up in front of that building," Hugh said, pointing to the place with the blue and white sign out the front. "The men will disconnect the equipment and start harvesting panels from the roof. It's dangerous work, so be careful to stand clear. I'll have them give you the information you will need to recommission the equipment safely in Gospers."

"These men know about this old technology?" Maia asked.

"They are our power crew, responsible for all repairs and maintenance of our wind turbines and other power infrastructure at the bridge. They have studied old texts about this equipment, including the solar panels, in case we ever have need. This complex is large, and has far more than you can take today, so they will ensure to isolate the area they take from the rest, so as not to shut it down. The lights of this place are a useful beacon for travellers."

Soon the men were passing panels from the roof of the building down to Hugh, who carefully stacked them, one after the other, in the back of the cart.

"Will the cart become too heavy?" Maia asked.

"These panels are not too heavy, at around twenty five to thirty kilograms. If we get twenty of them, it will be like four men, roughly. If you take it easy, it should be fine. The batteries are another man in weight at least. I'd suggest you don't rush to install them, you should study the technology a bit to figure out how best to position them. Once we have a road cleared, the boys can come and help with that."

"That would be greatly appreciated, I can assure you," Maia said. "The thought of my little village having electric lighting excites me. But I need to think about how best to distribute it. Do we put all the lights in the streets? Or in the houses?"

"I would suggest the streets to start with, to enable easy navigation around the village at night. If there is load to spare, focus that on public buildings or spaces. If there is still some to spare, then look at private houses. Remember, once the village is better connected by road, more can be retrieved for power to the individual homes later."

They were interrupted by shouting. Two of the men were running, waving arms in warning at the third, who was carrying a large object out of the building. Two long cables had dropped from the top, and were dragging behind the man, who had failed to notice.

As he stepped through a large glass doorway, the cables brushed a metal strip on the floor, and sparks exploded into the air, igniting the mans long hair as he dropped the thing he was carrying and ran. Hugh rushed to intercept him.

"Doug!" Hugh shouted, as the man found a water canteen in his bags and poured it over his own head. "Take care, you fool! Are you injured?"

"I, I, I... I'm f, fine," Doug replied.

"Good," Hugh said. "That could have been deadly. Be careful, man!"

"Sorry, Elder," Doug said, sitting on the ground.

"We'll have to leave that battery. We don't have time to check it over properly. I'll have the others fetch one from a different building," Hugh said.

Maia looked at Elly, concern in her eyes.

"If they're the ones who know what their doing, imagine if we tried this ourselves."

"So we wait for the men to reach your village," Elly said. "Like Hugh suggested."

The men sourced two more batteries, loaded them on the cart, and put Doug on the cart as well.

"If you copped any of that discharge, too much exercise will be bad for your heart right now," Hugh said.

They travelled slower returning to the bridge, and reached it after night fall. The woman elder was waiting at the gates as they arrived, and welcomed them with relief.

"This was a risky task, I'm glad to see everybody safe," she said. "Now you girls hurry inside. Miriam will take you to the dining hall. We will meet you there. I have some other matters to discuss with Hugh."

*   *   *

The Windsor militia troupe with Greg, Alex and Artemis in tow entered Paddy's Market after a good night's rest in one of the nearby buildings, which they were assigned to by the local militia when they arrived in the evening.

The local militia, who had been previously unwilling

to accept the wild story of a teenage boy, listened at last to the information Greg and the men from Windsor gave them about the thieves.

A man calling himself General Watterson listened intently as Daryl gave him the full account of what Windsor knew, from the abduction of Maia to the attempt to sell her at the market, her escape with Alex, and further detail regarding the activities of the group before the current situation.

"We do take thieves seriously. They have an impact on all traders, and on the commissions paid to the market precinct," the general said. "However the evidence has been slim that this was taking place. And the trafficking of people for sale is a serious allegation to add to those already levelled by your young companion against a group which regularly trades in our precinct."

"This man," Daryl said, pointing at Greg. "Can identify any produce recently sold here which may have been stolen from the trader out of Gospers village. Greg, please describe some of the products stolen."

"We had a selection of goods taken, along with the girl. Our village deals in preserved poultry meats and related poultry products, as well as herbs, spices, and in season vegetables."

"And how are we expected to confirm the produce is yours and not traded legitimately from some other village?"

"All our products are branded with a G, and the date we packaged it for trade."

"Even so, there may be other villages who use that branding."

"So you are asking us to prove our wares, but refusing to accept the proof?" Greg shouted, rising from his chair in anger.

"Greg, calm yourself." Daryl said, raising his hand, palm outward, as Greg simmered. "We are not asking for return of goods or commissions, it is too late for that. Any compensation if forthcoming, should come from the thieves themselves, not your precinct. Indeed, we intend to handle the arrest ourselves as well. If you can only advise where these men went after their business with the market was concluded?"

"Well, if that is the case," the general replied. "I can tell you that after concluding their business and securing payment for the dog, they left the markets, heading in the same direction from which they had returned with the boy in the days prior. In addition, given your compelling testimony, and in an effort to further support the relations between my own precinct and yours, should that group return, we will detain them and dispatch word to Windsor, that you may return and collect them for your own judicial procedures to be followed. Also, as their regular trading was delayed, they departed late in the evening yesterday, likely to camp nearby."

"Thank you, General Watterson," Daryl said, standing. "We will take our leave and continue our pursuit. I bid you well."

As they left, Greg was still fuming as he approached Daryl. They made their way out of the immense market building and onto the street. Daryl waved Alex ahead, to lead them as he knew the way.

"What the hell was that all about?" Greg snapped.

"Those men," Daryl explained. "They are not a true militia, enforcing law and justice. I suspect they were well aware of the girl's plight. They take a commission from every trade that passes through the markets. Every. Trade. I'm surprised they promised to detain the thieves, and I truly doubt they will."

"But, then, shouldn't we do something?"

"It would be pointless. At this time, I feel we must be thankful our quarry was delayed, and are now closer at hand. Besides, this militia is a foreign power to Windsor. We can not enforce our law in their territory. We got the information we need to continue, I suggest we instead focus on the task at hand. Such a lawless place is not something we can change with this small group of men."

Chapter 18 – Misdirection

The sun rose over a dewy morning at the Great Northern Hotel. Wendy was tidying the forecourt, wondering if any travellers would be passing today. A large group of traders had left the hotel the day before, three families from somewhere to the south, on their way home after trading to the north shore markets in Narrabeen.

As can be the case when the hotel is busy, not all of the cleaning occurred before bed, and now as the traders had left at first light, Wendy took the opportunity before breakfast of tidying things somewhat.

She was about to go inside, to the kitchen, and fetch herself breakfast, when she saw a group approaching from the direction of the city. She frowned as she stared intently at them, shielding her eyes from the morning sun with her left hand as she picked up a chair, rattling it against the table loudly.

"Nigel!" She called. "Come out here please, and bring as many as you can rouse."

Wendy removed her apron and brushed herself down, before arming herself with the mop. She walked forward, to the curb, and watched as the rough group approached the far side of the intersection. There were several men visible, pushing an ancient vehicle.

"It's just as the girl described," Wendy muttered as Nigel stepped alongside her, six others from inside grumbling as they secured their hastily donned clothing. "Nigel, be ready for a fight. We give these dogs nothing."

"Yes, Ma'am!"

The approaching group was halfway across the intersection, when they stopped. Two men stepped forward.

"This doesn't look like a welcome party, Boss." One of the men said.

"Shut up, Barry." The other snapped. "You there, we

are seeking a little thief who stole our horse. A young strap of a girl. Have you seen her come through here?"

Wendy forced herself to smile, stepping forward to meet the men, Nigel remaining close by her side.

"Why yes, we did see a girl child. We thought it odd that one like her would be travelling alone, and with such a fine horse. I daresay you must be keen to retrieve such a valuable animal. But alas, I fear you are rather too late."

"What do you mean, woman?" Boss snapped. "Spit it out."

"When the girl said she wished to visit Windsor, we directed her back the way you came. You see, the M2 is the fastest route to take for that destination. You crossed it not that far back. She'd be well on her way to Windsor by now. She has days of head start over you gentlemen."

"We move quickly enough, woman. We'll catch the pesky thief, and then she'll get the punishment she deserves."

"I'm sure she will, a big strong man like yourself would be..." Wendy's voice turned deep and menacing. "More than capable of defeating a little girl. You have your information, get out of my sight, you filthy scum, before my people see to it you never harm another girl again. That child will be almost to Windsor before you escape that highway. The tribes along that road will not take kindly to the likes of you. We already saw to that."

"Let's move, Barry." Boss snarled. "This bitch isn't going to help us out, and we have a lot of ground to make up if we're going to catch the girl. We'll deal with any tribes in our way as we find them. I'm sure they'd listen to us over some trumped up diva like that."

As the troupe of thieves returned the way they had come, Wendy pulled Nigel aside.

"Nigel, tail them, when you can, get ahead of them and make sure any of our friends in that direction are aware this group has been stealing girls. I want a warm welcome for our good friends in the SUV. And make sure anybody they ask continues the ruse that the girl went that way."

"Yes, Ma'am," Nigel said, running a short distance then ducking between some buildings.

Wendy smiled.

"Nigel knows these streets better than anybody. He'll reach the first tribe before they reach the highway. But be careful, Nigel, come home safe."

*   *   *

Maia sat with the bridge elders, as they poured over the maps in the book.

"Show me again child, where your Gospers village is." the woman elder said.

Maia pointed at the place on the map, far to the west.

"That's further north than ideal, but it still looks like this Melong place is the closest actual road connected town. If it's even a town today."

"I've never been there..." Maia said.

"Do not worry about that. What I am concerned with is establishing our trade route. Based on this map, I believe if you pass through Wisemans Ferry, where you will find another settlement, there is a second ferry, which was called Webbs Creek Ferry. If you cross that, then continue south west, following the roads on this map, you will eventually reach Putty Road. It will be a long journey, but Putty Road takes you north through Melong. The puzzle is how you get from there to your village."

"I can follow the creeks," Maia suggested. Once we get halfway from Melong, I can find my way."

"I have another suggestion," the woman said. "While I prefer we build a more direct route, in order to see you travel home safely, I suggest you continue north from Melong. Hugh advises us that there is a settlement in the vicinity of Putty Creek, and that there are still old roads there, not major ones, but still, roads that penetrate deep into the mountains."

'So you suggest I travel via there?" Maia asked. "I believe Uncle visited a place called Putty once, so it must be accessible."

"It must be, and perhaps somebody there can better direct you, though you will have your maps as well. It would likely be less distance than going via Windsor, and should your abductors be in pursuit, you are less likely to meet them this way."

"I'll ask in Wisemans Ferry if any know more of those roads," Maia said. "I know the map looks like a short distance, but the mountains are treacherous. It would be certain death for the unprepared. I'd rather make it home alive, than make it home fast."

"Wise words, young lady," the woman said. "Had you agreed readily, I may have been forced to consider sending a few men with you, which we can ill afford at this time. Or else I may have needed to forbid you travel, instead sending somebody to fetch you a companion to take you back home."

"I have travelled a long way already. I am capable of surviving this journey, and I will get back to Gospers. If I have to skirt around Windsor, so be it, but I should not have to risk my life in doing so."

'Very well. I will return your book to you now, and wish you well. See Miriam on your way out, she is preparing supplies for your journey."

"But you've already done so much!" Elly protested.

"Do not fret, child. We could not in good conscience let you travel without enough food to get you at least as far as a place to restock. What Miriam has prepared should get you as far as Melong, if you travel that way.

"Thank you," Maia said. "I hope our settlements can enjoy a long relationship from now on."

"As do we, child," the elder said.

* * *

The Windsor militia moved quickly, a sense of the prey being in reach spurring them to action. It was late afternoon when they reached The Great Northern Hotel. As they crossed the intersection, the men rested in the forecourt of the hotel, tired from their hard march. Daryl went and knocked on the large double doors.

"Hello?" Daryl called out. "We're looking for some information, and perhaps a place to rest."

"That depends on the information you require," a

woman's voice replied. "We may not be able to accommodate you, if we don't like what you have to ask."

At the sound of her voice, Artemis began to bark, excited at something she seemed to recognise, her tail whipping side to side as she rushed towards the door.

"Artemis! Stop!" Alex shouted, running to catch the pup.

"Artemis?" The woman said as the door opened. "If that dog is Artemis, then that boy must be Alex, am I correct?"

"Yes, I'm Alex."

"In that case, you are welcome, travellers. Please, come inside, I'll get some water on the boil, and you can enquire after what it is you seek."

Alex caught the dog, and turned to face Wendy.

"I'm sorry, ma'am, I don't know what got her so excited all of a sudden."

"I think I do. That dog was Maia's, and Maia spent a lot of time with Uncle, her mentor. I believe My voice is similar to his."

"Why would it be?" Alex asked, but she had already moved away, and was addressing Daryl directly.

"Now then, since you were the one to knock, I assume you are the leader of this group?"

"I am," Daryl replied. "I command the seventeenth troupe of the Windsor Militia. We are accompanied by Alex, and the dog, who you seem to already know, and this gentleman, who is from the village of Gospers, and seeks a girl who was abducted from there, to fulfil a promise to the girl's father."

"I see, so why does the militia accompany these two? A missing child is hardly your normal concern."

"We seek to capture the thieves who took the child, and stole the trade goods which were in her possession."

"Well, that explains a lot. I had suspected her to be from Gospers, though she never mentioned the village by name. And I can tell you you are heading in the right direction for the girl, but the wrong direction for the thieves."

"I'm not sure I understand?" Greg said.

"Oh, it's simple really. Maia and a new friend have taken their two horses and a cart and are heading home, the long way. They have taken the M1 motorway north, and will leave it to go via Wisemans Ferry, and back home via Windsor."

"And the thieves?" Daryl asked.

"I have seen them early this morning. I am quite surprised you have arrived so soon on their heals. They were not the most pleasant of men, and I directed them to Windsor via a quicker but much more dangerous route."

"That route?" Daryl asked. "It was the M2, wasn't it?"

"How do you know that?" Greg asked. "And what is this M2?"

"The M2 is a major highway we crossed this afternoon. I've heard of it many times, but never travelled it. Between here and the city, it traverses the Lane Cove Tunnel, one of the most dangerous tunnels in the entire city area due to the violence of the tribe who have settled there. They are famous far and wide for their ruthlessness. That tribe run a fair distance along the m2, mingling for trade with other similar gangs along it's way. On some occasions, those gangs run raids into territory protected by the Windsor Militia. If those men act in the wrong way on that road, there may not be much left for us to apprehend when we do catch up. And we certainly do not want to be out on that road after dark."

"Then it is good that Maia went a longer way," Greg said.

"It is," Daryl replied, turning back to Wendy. "Miss, would your hotel have rooms sufficient for my men? And we can pay for food and drink as well."

"Since it is for Maia's benefit," Wendy said, smiling at Alex and the dog. "I can provide accommodation. I assume I will be billing it to the Militia. There will be a communal dinner in the dining hall at seven. I will show you to your rooms, you can freshen up, but be sure to arrive in time to eat. You'll hear the bell when it's ready, but if possible, you should be downstairs before then to get a good seat."

Chapter 19 – Roads

Maia gently stroked Barry's neck, her slow fingers almost nestling in his shaggy mane. The sun barely crested the eastern horizon, casting long morning shadows across the bridge. Barry snorted, steam rising from his nostrils as a small group approached them.

It was three days since they collected the panels and returned, and life in the bridge seemed almost normal to Maia. She turned to look along the bridge, as Elly and the elders approached.

"You're keen to leave," Elly said.

"Well, not really," Maia replied. "It's just..."

"I know, we have a long road ahead."

"No," Maia said. "It's not that. I wonder if we should..."

"If we should go?" Elly said, taken aback. "Of course we should. You have to get home."

"But is it worth it? Risking our lives to climb the mountain, when these people have built such a perfect home right here, no risk..."

"And no family. Not yours anyway."

"I know. But I don't know if I can make it. I'm getting tired, Elly."

"Of course you can. Barry knows it, look at him. Well rested and ready. Same for Farrow. I know she'll take me anywhere, now she's rested."

"You don't have to come," Maia said.

"Of course I do."

"No, you don't. I appreciate the help and the company, but when it comes down to it, we're not returning to your family, are we? You could stay here, it'd make no difference for you, this is a nice home."

"Maia," Elly said, lowering her eyes. "You idiot. You're my only family now."

Elly walked to Farrow, and the horse reached her head

down to welcome the girl.

"And you of course, Farrow," Elly said. "I always wanted a sister I could ride with. Now I found one. I love it here, I want to visit again…"

Elly turned and stood in front of Maia, staring her in the eyes with a determined stance and a firm expression.

"But I'm not letting you out of my sight, now I've found you."

Tears welled in Maia's eyes and she embraced her adoptive sibling, shaking her head slightly as she drew away again.

"Of course you won't," Maia said. "And I'm glad. I've wanted a sister as well."

"Girls," Hugh said, shattering the moment. "You won't be alone, not initially. Given our trade mission to Brooklyn is out of the question, I now have urgent business with the small settlement at Peats Ridge. So I will accompany you that far."

"They had traders going as well?" Maia asked.

"No, but our traders would normally stop by and take goods on their behalf. With that no longer possible, they will need to make other arrangements. I hope to assist them in that regard."

"I see," Maia said. "Then we will welcome your escort."

Miriam and two of the young men of the bridge approached, carrying large sacks. Wordlessly, they placed them in the cart, and one of the men secured them in place with a length of rope.

"That," Hugh said, "should be enough provisions to get you to Windsor, or perhaps home. Or at worst, to offer in trade if necessary along the way."

"Thank you," Maia said. "You've all been too kind."

"We are glad to help, child," The woman elder said. "It means new opportunities for all of us. Once you reach Gospers and have the trade route established. I look forward to eating fried eggs again. Given you have poultry there, I hope you have those as well?"

"We do, but we don't trade them much, transport is too difficult."

"We will have our engineers look into a way of solving that," the woman said. "Or perhaps you could trade some hens for a pig?"

"Perhaps we can," Maia replied with a smile.

By the time the sun was above the horizon, they were on their way, the brisk morning air refreshing and the sunshine warming. A low fog was lifting from the valley below the bridge as they climbed the hill to the south, and before long passed over the crest. The bridge, so welcome and hospitable, was left behind.

Maia wondered briefly if they would ever see it again. The warmth of the sun was a bright, welcome relief punctuated by the cool shade from the cuttings as they made their way back towards Peats Ridge Road.

'Maia,' Hugh said. "I have been thinking about the journey ahead. I think it would be foolish to go across unknown terrain. You know well how treacherous the mountains can be."

"Yes, they are dangerous to those not familiar, that is certain."

"I know you were considering going cross country from Melong. Have you ever been there?"

"No..."

"Neither have I. I worry that there may be no town there at all. If you can't replenish your supplies for the journey, cutting across wild lands from there is almost certainly a fatal decision."

"Then I will ask at Wisemans Ferry. Perhaps they will have a better idea of that place. If not, then we can simply go to Windsor. The roads go that far don't they?"

"They do, and they are well travelled. And you know your way home from there, don't you?"

'I do..."

"Then I would recommend that route above all else. You can have your people commence the construction of a new route from your home. Nobody needs to lose their lives over it."

"You're right, of course," Maia said. "And Windsor was my original goal. My only concern is lack of funds to pay for food and accommodation. Windsor is not a cheap place outside of the peak trading season, and I fear we may not arrive until then."

"Do not concern yourself. The market at Windsor is a signed representative of the Trader's Guild of The Eastern Seaboard. I am a member. I will give you a promissory note. Present it in the market and they will take care of you."

"But that means you'll have to pay, right?" Elly said.

"Yes, but we can sort those details out another time. Gospers and the bridge will be trading partners soon, after all."

* * *

Greg glanced back at the overpass above the M2, wondering if this was a wise course of action. Daryl had insisted they leave the boy and the dog behind, due to the danger. Greg wondered if he should have pushed to stay as well. But Daryl implied he was needed, so here he was. Regretting the militia's need for extra men.

The sun was warm, striking low from the east as they passed between the long shadows. Houses and trees lined the road, hiding who knew what dangers. The men from Windsor glanced around in apprehension, jumping at any shadow which moved in the gentle breeze.

Daryl called them to a halt, to mingle on the road, sitting ducks to any gangs nearby. Greg watched as Daryl sent a man ahead, to scout the road for danger, or a place to rest.

"Daryl," Greg said. "Are we sure we want to stop here?"

"Yes," Daryl replied. "I believe we have arrived on the wrong road."

"Why?" Greg asked.

"We have not yet been ambushed. And I believe the tunnel is beneath us at this point. But if we made such an error, our prey may have done the same."

"But what if they didn't?" Greg asked.

"We have no way of knowing, but if they did not enter the tunnel, and we do, we will likely face a tougher fight than if we were pursuing an enemy. The gangs in the tunnels might forgive us if we have a reason. If we can't prove we do, they'll kill without hesitation."

"Then what's the plan?" Greg asked.

"I would like to find a safe place to set up a camp off the road. We have no way of knowing what places the local gangs frequent. If the scout can find the right place to stop, we can send smaller parties out to look for our prey from there. A marching army is worthless if it's exhausted when it catches the enemy."

A short time later, the scout returned. He was running hard, and Daryl helped him onto a horse before allowing him to make his report.

"There is evidence of a skirmish on the road, and not far from there an open field which sees little traffic. A sign says it is Tantallon Oval. It is separated from the road by an overgrown garden. We will be out of sight there."

"An ancient sports ground then, it will suffice. Men, move out!"

The group moved quickly, and soon found the place the scout had spoken of. The road had scuffs in the dirt as expected from a fierce battle between two groups. There were no bodies.

"The site has been cleaned up reasonably well," Daryl said. "And from the marks, I would guess it was a stalemate and both parties withdrew. One along the road and one into the east, through the trees and houses."

"Then the ones we want went along the road," Greg said.

"Correct," Darryl replied. "And with substantial injuries, they are likely to be moving slowly. I'll send another scout. They might be slow, but they still have a head start over us. We can rest here while we assess the situation."

*   *   *

Barry strained as he dragged the SUV to the side of the road. The rest of the men lay exhausted on the ground. They had all fought hard, but were spent after a sound beating at the hands of the local gang.

"Boss, if we get attacked again, we're done for. We need a safer place."

"There isn't one," Boss replied. "We're in a bad spot, I'll grant you that, but we need rest. And so do those who attacked us. We might be in a bad way, but we aren't dead, or prisoners, and neither were they. I would say those others are likely resting as well, just as battered as we are. And those gangs are territorial. If we continue, we might meet a fresh enemy, but for now, those men are not going to attack again. So we stay here. No enemy will come for us while we recover."

"I hope you're right, boss," Barry said. "But something else bothers me. That girl."

"I know, I feel the same," Boss said. "Either she's dead, or she never came this way."

"The woman lied?"

"Probably," Boss said. "But maybe not."

"What do you mean?"

"I've heard of this place. We should be in a tunnel now, if we'd taken the road she said."

'I see. So, what's the plan?"

"I don't know. Maybe we need to go back. Or perhaps we should just forget the whole deal. We can't afford any more of this bullshit."

"Get some rest, boss. We can talk about it again later."

*   *   *

Greg met the scout on his return, only a couple of hours later.

"Get Daryl," the scout said. "I found them. I scouted for others, on the way back but there were none. They look properly beaten up. We should go take them now, while they aren't rested."

"I heard," Daryl said, walking up to them. "We head out now. It's not noon yet, we can get back here with our prisoners before dark, and then back the way we came. The local gang likely won't attack tonight, since they've just had a stalemate, they're hopefully in similar condition to the bandits."

The camp was struck in record time, and the militia men left at a good pace, intent on their prey. The villainous group was finally in reach.

Chapter 20 – The Ferry

Maia drove the cart down from the Pacific Motorway onto Peats Ridge Road. This road was far more dilapidated than the motorway, but it still showed signs of regular traffic. The road was wide, and clear. The cart bounced along its rough surface, but it was still an acceptable route. The horses had no difficulty.

They soon passed a side road, with a sign indicating a quarry nearby. A man was walking towards them from that side road, so Maia stopped the cart.

"Where are you headed, strangers?" the man asked.

"Wisemans Ferry," Maia replied. "Up through Central Mangrove."

"That'll get you there," the man replied. "But why that way? You can cut several hours by taking the trade route. Our village in the quarry goes to Wisemans Ferry often. Do you have a map?"

"Yes," Elly replied, digging out the book before Maia could stop her.

"Excellent, show me that," the man said, reaching for the book as Hugh reached and took it instead.

Hugh opened to the relevant page and pointed.

"See? We follow this road up, then come back along Wisemans Ferry Road. It's a long way, but we have time."

"That's wrong," the man said, pointing at a place on the map. "See this line? That's Cooks Road. It's not a big road, but it's passable. Our traders go that way. It leads to Popran Road, which winds about a bit, but takes you straight across, instead of going all that way north only to turn around and come south again. Cuts about fifty kilometres off your journey. These old maps were made for cars, and they show the better roads. Sure, the smaller roads are probably mostly gone now, but that one, as I say, our traders use it, so it's well maintained."

"This is good advise, Maia." Hugh said. "This man is

142

from the village I intended to visit, and they can be trusted. Their advice on a better route was one of the reasons I wanted to come along."

"Thank you, then," Maia replied. "You've saved us some time."

"What settlements remain along that route?" Hugh asked the man.

"None, though a family lives at the old Pure Valley guest house, a short walk from the road at Mangrove Creek. They keep to themselves. Best to push on to the Ferry. That's about an eight hour walk, less with the horses, if you keep a good pace."

"Good," Hugh said. "Then I feel safe to leave these girls to their journey. If you would escort me into your village, I'd be grateful."

"Of course, Sir," The man replied as Hugh returned the book to Elly and the man bowed with a tip of his hat. "A pleasure to meet you both, ladies."

"Thank you, kind sir," Maia replied, flicking the reigns and driving the cart away.

A short time later, they turned left onto Cooks road, and the landscape became progressively wilder as they travelled deeper into the mountains. Soon the road turned a sharp left then right, at an intersection of several smaller tracks, with a large stone sign that read "Glenworth Valley."

Maia paused for a moment, examining the trails, before looking again at the map in the book. With a frown, she selected the most well travelled looking of the trails, and they were under way again. They crossed a creek, and shortly after found another intersection. Following the busier trail, Maia turned left and they continued.

Trees grew tall and close, but the road was reasonably smooth. It wound its way through the forest, the sunlight barely penetrating the trees. They travelled for hours, until they reached an intersection, where the road met another at a sharp hairpin. A rough painted sign pointed the direction to Wisemans Ferry and a rough foot trail led down to a creek below the new road. Maia stopped on the turn, the sunshine hitting them with full force for the first time since they started on this old road, and reached for the bags.

"I think it's time for lunch," Maia explained as Elly looked at her quizzically. "Take a bucket to the water will you? The horses must be parched."

Elly unhitched Barry, and led both horses around the bend, to a small patch of long grasses, then clambered down to the creek to fetch water. It was slow work down the hillside, but she made it back in one piece. Maia prepared sandwiches from the preserved meats and bread in their pack, given to them by the people of the bridge.

Sitting on the cart, the girls ate, the horses nibbling the grass and taking turns at the bucket. After a short while, Elly hitched Farrow to the cart, and tied Barry to the leading line from the back. Elly took the driver's seat and they set off into the afternoon.

*   *   *

The militia stormed the bandit's improvised camp, catching them unprepared, and found little resistance left in the men. Chaining the bandits together, the Militia led them back to Tantallon Oval, where the camp was set for the night.

The Bandits seemed almost relieved to have been captured, they had been so thoroughly broken by their battle with the gang. Once everything was set up, Daryl ordered the bandits brought to him one at a time. Boss was first.

He entered the tent where Daryl ordered him to his knees. Boss spat at the Militia man's feet, but had no strength for further rebellion. In response, Daryl hit him, a back handed slap across the face which sent him sprawling. The man's wounds were many, and he screamed involuntarily at the fall.

"Are you the leader of your group?"

"Yes."

"Do you deny raiding traders on route to Windsor?"

"Why would I do that?" Boss replied, knowing his words would not save him. "I mean, you've already judged us guilty. But on what basis?"

"We know of your group's activities. Your SUV is a recognisable thing, you know. We know you were raiding in the south last season. We know you decided to move north. We know about the girl, and the dog, and we know you took her with you through Blackheath. Do you deny this?"

Boss hung his head. He did not have the will to argue.

"We also know you intended to sell the girl in the city. Do you deny this?"

Boss said nothing. Daryl slapped him again, then waited for the man to get back up to his knees.

"Your silence is damning. I almost wish you hadn't encountered that gang before we caught up to you. I would have welcomed the chance to break you. Out of my sight, scum. You'll be sentenced in Windsor."

Two Militia men entered the tent. Boss was dragged from the tent, and Barry was thrown in.

"On your knees!" Daryl shouted.

Barry Complied.

"Name?" Daryl demanded.

"Barry. I won't say more."

"You don't need to," Daryl snapped, then reached out a hand. "On your feet, man. I know who you are. I know what you did."

"You know?"

"You helped the girl. And the name Barry is one I have heard before this season as well. I know about your brother, and your promise. And I know about your work undercover for the Blackheath Militia. It was a shame they disbanded when they did. But that made you a greater asset to the law, because your unit doesn't even exist, so how could you be a traitor to these bandits?"

"You are very well informed," Barry said. "You'll need to keep me in chains until Windsor."

"Of course, we wouldn't want to break your cover. But are these the ones who did it?"

"Boss is the man who killed her, yes. I will be relieved to see him brought in. Once we reach Windsor, I will give testimony regarding all of his crimes. Then my dear sister will finally get some form of justice."

"It has taken many years. Not many men could have continued as you did."

"Killing that man would only have made me the same as he is. But becoming trusted enough for this betrayal to have it's full effect, that is the essence of revenge."

"Remind me never to cross you. I will not tell my men, so that they continue to treat you as one of the bandits. That way you can keep your cover as long as possible."

"I would appreciate that."

"Now then, back into character," Daryl said, before shouting. "Get out of my sight, you worthless bastard!"

*   *   *

As the sun was setting, Maia and Elly were driving the cart alongside a wide river, as they approached Wisemans Ferry. Lights reflected across the water from the settlement, and the girls could see the ferry, attached to both banks of the river with long cables, a tall tower on either side. As they approached, the ferry crossed to meet them.

It moved in near total silence, just a faint whirring and the sounds of the water slapping against the hull. They reached the foot of the tower and a young man met them. The road turned down an ancient concrete ramp into the water.

"Welcome, travellers. I'm Nico. You're lucky to arrive now. The ferry stops in half an hour."

"How does it move so quietly?" Elly asked.

"It's electric," the young man proclaimed with pride. "My father set it up. We used to have turnstiles pulled by horses on either side. Now we use the turnstiles to lift heavy stones up the towers, and then hook them to a different pulley at the top, and as they lower back down, they turn a generator which creates electricity we store in batteries at the base of the tower. That electricity powers the ferry and the town lights. We stop the ferry to conserve power through the night, so the lights stay on and in case of emergency."

"That's clever!" Maia said. "But don't the rocks fall too fast?"

"We slow them with a series of breaks and pulleys. They come down slowly, and generate plenty of power when they do. I tend to hoist this stone three or four times an hour. When I go home, we rely on the battery for the night, which is why we have to stop the ferry."

"It's a clever way to make power," Elly said. "Since there isn't a lot of sun or wind down in the valley here."

The ferry arrived, and a second young man jumped off to tie it up and lower a plank to meet the ramp. The two young men helped them guide the horses and the cart onto the ferry, and then raised the plank, before casting off. The river was like glass, except where the ferry ploughed through it's surface. There was little noise, the dark night was a quiet mystery as they crossed.

"So where you two headed?" Nico asked.

"Windsor, then home," Maia replied. "It's been a long journey."

"I'd like to hear about it, if you don't mind?" the man asked. "I never get to travel, but I see a lot of travellers. I'll buy you a meal at the inn in exchange."

"A proper meal would be nice..." Elly said.

"OK then, I'll tell you the story," Maia said, smiling through weary eyes.

A short while later, the ferry was docked and the young men helped them to disembark. Maia looked at the second tower, still marvelling at the ingenuity of the people of this village, in constructing such a thing.

"It is pretty neat, isn't it?" Nico said.

"Yes, it's a clever way to solve the electricity problem. A lot of places still haven't got any power, and this would help them a lot."

"It's a shame we don't have plans for them," Nico said. "My father designed it, I helped him build it, but none of it was ever written down. He traded for the batteries and the turbines in the city."

"Then perhaps you need to travel, to build them or teach about it to other villages? I'm sure they'd pay you well for it," Maia said.

"That's a good idea, if I had somebody to work the towers and ferry here for a while. I might suggest it to my father. It might bring some nice trade goods to the village. Though I can see solar panels in your cart, I'd guess your home wouldn't be needing a tower then."

"Not immediately, but I'm sure we can think of a few places that would pay for your expertise just the same."

Chapter 21 – Roads To Windsor

The bandits walked heads down, arms chained, in a long line. They were attached at the ankles, guarded on all sides by the militia men. Daryl rode up front, with Greg by his side. The two men talked softly.

"So we should accompany you back to Windsor?" Greg said.

"Yes," Daryl replied. "The boy will be able to provide testimony to their identity and the fact they were seeking to recapture the girl. That testimony will make it easier to convict them in Windsor and have them sentenced accordingly."

"They'll recognise the boy when we collect him and the dog," Greg remarked.

"Does it matter? They already know we know about the girl and the dog. If they think the boy told us, it's fine. He wasn't ever their friend, after all."

"I suppose that's true..."

"Don't worry, mountain man. The boy will come to no harm."

"And once we have both given our testimony in Windsor, we can get back to looking for Maia. I still have a promise to keep."

"Yes, you may then be excused. Do you suppose you can find her quickly?"

"I don't know. I mean, we know she went past the Great Northern Hotel, they told us she was going north. But her path from there could diverge a number of ways. And we don't have a proper map."

"We will check that settlement Nigel told us about is properly, um," Daryl paused, a thoughtful look on his face. "Taken care of. As far as we know, they are the reason the girl went north. Perhaps that will free up a faster route for you to catch up to her. From Windsor you can retrace towards that place and take the road directly to her, instead of fighting your way through less passable routes and possibly missing her."

"I'd appreciate that," Greg replied. "If it means a quicker journey, it will help a lot."

The bridge over the M2, which they now knew was actually over this other surface road with the tunnel beneath, loomed large in the late afternoon shadows. They approached with some apprehension, knowing the local gangs could still attack at any moment. As they made their way onto the ramp to go up, they saw three men standing at the top, blocking their path.

"You there," one of the men shouted as they approached, wicked blades drawn. "What business do you have here?"

"I am Daryl, and I command this militia squad out of Windsor. We have pursued these bandits for many days, until we caught them along this road. We intend to return them to Windsor where they will face trial."

"You steal our quarry so lightly," the man said. "We had already fought them once for their trespass on our territory. Why should we not now fight you for the same crime? Those men are to be dealt with by our customs."

"My apologies for our trespass," Daryl replied. "But with the scent of their blood in our minds, our only concern was to capture these thugs before they repeated their crimes, regardless of if they committed them against our own people, or yours. Windsor does not leave it's problems for others to solve."

"Well spoken, militia man. But of what crimes do you find these men guilty?"

"Our courts will try them as highwaymen, for theft, murder, abduction, and the trafficking of young girls and women taken during those activities."

"I see," the man replied, still holding his sword high.

He paused, and then approached, slowly lowering the sword as he looked along the line of prisoners. He then returned to his companions, and addressed Daryl.

"None of these men are known to us, aside from the recent confrontation. If you have business with them for the crimes you have stated, then you do us a favour by removing such men from our lands. This is unusual, but we will allow you to pass. Do not expect such lenience should the same occur another time."

"Understood," Daryl said. "We are grateful for your understanding on this occasion. I will ensure Windsor is aware of your cooperation, and the favour will be returned if such need should ever arise."

"Good," the man replied. "Well met, men of Windsor. I wish you well on your journey escorting your villains to trial."

"One more thing," Greg said. "I am not of Windsor, but accompany these men in seeking a girl who was stolen from the village of Gospers. Have you seen any sign of such a girl? She will have been riding a large horse at this time, I believe."

"Such a girl was seen by our scout crossing this bridge some days ago, heading towards the west. We know no more of her, she did not return this way."

"Thank you, that confirms what we had been told by others further west. I am grateful."

"We wish you good fortune finding your missing child, man of Gospers," the man said. "Now, we must ask you not delay. The hunting parties will soon begin their evening patrol, and they will be less inclined to allow you to pass."

"Thank you, men of the tunnel."

"We are men of the cove. The tunnel is only part of our territory. It will serve you well to remember this."

"We will. Fair well."

Daryl led his men, and the prisoners, up the ramp and turned west. By sundown, they arrived at the Great Northern Hotel, where Wendy greeted them. Boss and his men were not welcome inside, so Daryl set up his camp in the road, and they waited out a long night, the men taking shifts guarding the prisoners until the dawn light crept over the eastern horizon.

With camp struck, they were gone before breakfast.

*   *   *

Maia stood on the verandah of the inn at Wisemans Ferry, watching the dawn light slowly crest the trees. Elly came to stand beside her, watching the colours dance in the morning dew.

"This is a beautiful place, isn't it?" Elly said.

"Every place is, if you allow it to be," Maia replied. "Beauty and ugliness both come from inside people, not from landscapes."

"That's deep," Elly said.

"It's something Uncle once told me. I think I understand it now."

"But if the place has only ugliness from the hearts of its people, it can only become an ugly place," Elly said. "Well, that's what I think anyway."

"Do you want to stay here?"

"I wouldn't mind, for a while, but I don't need to. We stopped for a while at the bridge, after all. But this reminds me of home. My real home. Before it became ugly there."

"What happened? If you don't mind my asking."

"No," Elly said. "No, it's OK. But I have tried not to remember for so long, it seems perverse to try to remember now."

"If you don't want to tell me..."

"No, I do, but I don't know where to start."

"Then take your time. We have all the time in the world, remember?"

"Of course we do. But it's like, secrets are lies between friends. So I want to tell you. Growing up, I loved that place. It was quiet, pretty, and my parents were kind, loving people."

"Were?"

"I had to bury them myself. Those bastards raided the village. There were only five houses, we were a close knit group, just living our lives, until they arrived. They set up camp in the middle of our fields. They ruined our crops, burnt it all. My father, and one of the other men went to them to ask them to leave. They refused, killing the other man without hesitation."

"That's terrible..."

"It was only the start. They stayed there for weeks, and

things started to go missing from our houses. There was no militia, no strong men to help us. The people of my village, my family and friends, they learned hatred from those bastards. I learned hatred from them. It made our hearts ugly. We all wanted them to die, if they wouldn't leave. Then my father found our entire winter store of food had been taken. Furious, he went and spoke to them."

Elly stopped talking. She sat on the edge of the verandah, and bowed her head. Tears splashed on her knees. Maia sat beside the girl, and wrapped an arm around her shoulders.

"They murdered him, without a second thought. They killed my father, then dragged his body behind a horse. After they dumped him outside our house, they set about destroying everything. They murdered the entire village that night, and burnt it all to the ground. They had made the place ugly, and now they destroyed what was left."

"How did you escape?"

"I was with Farrow, behind the house when they returned, dragging my father. I couldn't do anything to stop them. When they dragged out my mother, and cut off her head, I screamed, and I thought I was done for, but the neighbour, my aunt, screamed at the same time, and they went for her. Then they took my little brother, and they cut him to pieces while he screamed. I ran. I got on Farrow, and I ran into the forest. I returned the next day, and they were gone. I buried everybody as best I could, it took three days to dig the graves and bury them all. The ground was too hard for me, so the graves weren't deep enough. I had to find rocks and dirt to pile on top. On the third day, those other people found me there. I was too exhausted and upset to fight them off. They took me and farrow, and it was about a month later they set up in that place where you found me. I'd been with them a year by then."

"Elly..." Maia said, then heard sobbing, not from the other girl.

Maia turned, and saw the land lady standing in the doorway to their room, hands covering her face as tears of sympathy poured from her wrinkled eyes.

"I'm sorry girls, I shouldn't have been listening. But

your story... I'm so sorry. Stay here as long as you need. I'll talk to my husband. He won't ask for money, or anything else. With what you've been through... You poor children. That this is what our world has become. Don't worry about coming to the dining room, I'll bring you some breakfast shortly."

The girls sat in silence for several minutes, both weeping as Elly covered her eyes with her hands. Finally Maia stood, and led the other girl back inside, settling her into a chair by a dresser, she began to brush her hair.

"You have a new home now," Maia said. "Wherever I am, whatever I'm doing, that's your home from now on."

*   *   *

Nigel accompanied the Militia as far as the walled settlement. The gates stood open, and there was an eerie quiet.

"We came back after the girls left, and put a bit of fear into them," Nigel explained.

They entered, and searched, but there was no sign of the people who had lived there until recently.

"It's a shame, if they were abducting people to fill their settlement, it would have been useful to have them somewhere we could deal with them. Now they could be anywhere."

"When we returned, the old lady who led them seemed unwell," Nigel said. "If they lost her, and left this secure place, I doubt they'll provide the same threat to anybody they once did. That old woman was the one pushing them to do those things."

"I see," Daryl replied. "If she ruled them with fear, the group may have disbanded. We will have to keep our eyes and ears open, in case they do settle elsewhere and start to do the same things again."

"I will return to the hotel now," Nigel said. "Safe travels to Windsor. And Alex, I hope you and the pup are reunited with the girl soon."

"Thank you," Alex replied. "I'm sure Greg will be pleased to get her home."

Nigel left, and the militia led their captives without further mishap. Daryl drove them hard, and the militia men could feel the reward of home in their bones. They hiked for nearly ten hours that day, and entered Windsor as the moon lit the evening sky.

With the prisoners secured, the men returned to their homes, while Daryl arranged an evening's barracks accommodation for Greg, Alex and Artemis.

Chapter 22 – Next steps

Maia and Elly chose to stay another day in Wisemans Ferry. After letting out her emotions about what happened to her family, Elly needed the time to regain her composure, and her emotional strength to take on the rest of the journey They sat in the dining area of the hotel that evening, joined by Nico and the land lady.

"I've been thinking about what you said," Nico said. "I want to travel, and take my knowledge of the power towers to other places, but I feel I need to learn more about electricity first. And I need to find somebody to take over my work here as well."

"If you want to study electricity, you should go to the bridge. They have a lot of knowledge about it there," Elly said.

"Do they know more than we do here?" Nico asked.

"I don't know about that," Maia said. "But they recovered the solar panels and batteries for us, and they have power from wind turbines and batteries running their entire settlement. So it couldn't hurt to at least go and see what they are doing."

"Thanks, I'll do that," he replied.

"And what will you girls do now?" the landlady asked.

"That hasn't changed," Maia said. "We continue to Windsor, and from there travel to my home at Gospers Village."

"That's in the mountains, isn't it? To the west?"

"Yes. We hope to establish a more direct route east to the bridge, and the other settlements in the area, but my first priority is getting home."

"Are there many settlements near yours?"

"Not nearby, but we have routes to those in the west of the mountains, and of course to Windsor. Opening new trade routes to the east can only help us out, and our produce doesn't seem to get far beyond Windsor."

"What produce is that?"

"We farm poultry. We send preserved chicken meat, jerky, and spices down to Windsor each season. As well as any excess vegetable produce which can make the journey."

"I believe I have tried your jerky when I was in Windsor last year. It was a good product. We don't have chickens here. Our settlement has a handful of pigs, like your friends at the bridge, but mostly we produce vegetables, a small amount of grain for bread to provide for ourselves, and alcohol for trade. If we could trade directly with Gospers for jerky, I think it would improve our dietary selection in both directions. I'm sure we could produce more food stuff for trade, if it came to that."

"When we have our new roads through the mountains, I'm sure we can arrange a stop here along the way," Maia assured her. "And if you make whisky here, I am pretty certain Uncle, my mentor at Gospers, has already spoken fondly of your produce."

"Indeed we do," the landlady said. "I am glad to hear our reputation for good whisky has made it up the mountain."

After a good meal, and lengthy discussions on matters of trade, travel, and gossip about the various people they had seen on their journey so far, Maia and Elly retired for the evening, ready to continue their journey the next day.

*   *   *

Greg and Alex gave a full and detailed report to the leaders of the militia. They began their long walk to the M1 with Artemis at first light. They took with them rations to last a few days, and were intent on making the best time possible.

With barely a ten minute break for lunch, and stops for toileting along the way, they walked with haste and reached the start of the motorway in the early evening.

"It seems strange, doesn't it?" Alex mused.

"What does?" Greg asked.

"That long walk, and so few people along it."

"People are superstitious. Any settlements along that route may have been hard hit by the viruses a century ago, and people still avoid the area."

"Even so..."

"I believe Wendy said they have many travellers stop at The Great Northern, on their way into the city. Perhaps her premises reduces the necessity for stops before Windsor?"

"Or perhaps the militia haven't always been so strong at defending the settlements in the area. How far do you suppose the lane cove tunnel group raids?"

"As I understand it, the area controlled by gangs has been reducing in the north, and is one of the things that brought the bandit groups from the south into the area. Perhaps people will settle more places, if the militia remains strong and the area becomes known to be safe."

"Wendy and her family have held their home on their own."

"I wouldn't discount the struggles they likely have faced at times with the gangs. Or worse."

"Do you think there are more settlements away from the main highways?" Alex wondered.

"I have no doubt that's where the majority of them are. Gospers was settled because it was safer to be remote. Once we get away from the highway, I think we will encounter several smaller settlements in a day's walking."

"I hope so," Alex said. "That will mean more chances for Maia to have found help if she needed it."

"And more chances for trouble," Greg said. "We should be careful. We don't know if a settlement is friendly to outsiders just because it's not on the highway."

"I guess so. I hope Maia is safe."

"Have faith in that girl. You know how resourceful and determined she can be."

*   *   *

Leaving early in the morning, Maia and Elly travelled out of Wisemans Ferry along River road. It was a rough road, but passable. The ancient tar had long since been weathered away, and the people of the Wisemans Ferry settlement had maintained it as a dirt road for several kilometres.

The landlady ensured they were stocked up on food and water, insisting that the girls would need as much as she could fit into the cart.

The road twisted and wound its way through the unyielding landscape, and sometimes the girls felt despair that they were getting anywhere at all. By late morning, they found themselves at an intersection, where an ancient steel sign was barely legible. On it, the words "Leetsvale Caravan Park" could be made out only with extraordinary effort. A small grassy area sat by the roadside where the sign stood, and they took advantage of the opportunity to rest.

While the horses fed on the grass, the girls sat on the ground and nibbled lazily on some jerky from their supplies. Elly idly pulled blades of grass and tore them up, staring at the old sign. Finally, she spoke.

"Maia, do you suppose there are any gangs out here, like the ones in the city?"

"There could be," Maia said. "Remember, I was still in the mountains when those men found me."

"That's why I'm a little scared. What do you suppose happened to those men?"

"I don't know, but I think we left them far behind. I doubt they will be following us here."

"I hope you're right, Maia. I really do."

Elly stood, and walked to the sign. She touched it lightly, rust crumbling away from her fingers.

"They were probably so proud of this place, once upon a time. Now there's probably nothing there at all."

"Life can be like that," Maia said, walking to stand beside her friend. "A lot of places stop being anything special, and nature takes them back."

"Yeah, like home. My village will be like this Leetsvale place now, empty save for the animals. But the city hasn't been taken back."

"It will be, in time. I mean, look how the trees and grasses were swallowing up some of those houses? And those were along the main roadways. Imagine what it might be like away from the highways?"

"You're right, I guess," Elly said. "It just seems so unfair. I mean, there will be nothing left to remind travellers of my village. Not even a sign, like this one."

"One day, we can go back there and put a sign up if you like."

"No," Elly said, pausing in thought for several breaths. "No, I don't think I want to do that. Let it be a memory. My personal memory. There's nobody else left to care about it anyway."

Elly walked to the horses and took Farrow by the bridle, leading her to the cart, where she hooked the horse up. Maia retrieved Barry, and tethered him to the back.

"We should get a move on, just in case," Elly said. "If there are any gangs around, we don't want to stop outside a town."

They made slow progress as the weathered road wound its way south, until it reached an intersection. The girls turned onto Sackville Ferry Road as the sun was setting, but still they pushed on. Before long they arrived at a river, with no bridge. A long cable ran into the water, and a large flat barge slowly made its way towards them.

Smoke billowed from a smoke stack on the thing, and an old man yelled as it scraped up onto the bank of the road.

"You ladies crossing tonight? This will be my last trip."

"Please, if we may."

"It'll cost you, enough for a couple of meals if you have it to spare."

"I'm sure we can spare some food, if that'll do?" Maia asked.

"Good enough," the man said.

They soon made it safely to the other side, and the man ambled to the back of the cart.

"So what you got here?"

"Supplies from Wisemans Ferry," Maia said.

"Oh, well now, I don't suppose they'd have given youngsters like you some of that whisky?"

Maia shook her head.

"A shame, that. Oh well," the man said as he rummaged in their supplies. "I'll just take some of this then, and you can be off."

The man took enough food for a couple of day's meals, but the girls allowed it. The landlady had stocked them up so much, and Maia half suspected this was why. Waving goodbye as the ferry returned to the far side, the girls continued into the dusk.

As dusk gave way to night, Maia turned the cart off the road and into the overgrown yard of an old abandoned house, beside a fenced property with a sign which announced "Ebeneezer Public School." They secured the horses by manoeuvring the cart across the open space where a gate had once stood, then went into the old house, seeking shelter.

There was little of interest in the house, except for one room, in which a tall, narrow bookcase stood against the wall, well stocked with books on all manner of topics, including many fiction titles with all manner of unbelievable images on their faded and worn covers. Bizarre creatures, stars, planets, and strange, floating vehicles.

"What are they?" Elly wondered, idly flicking through one ancient paperback.

"It was called Science Fiction," Maia replied. "Uncle told me about it. But I never read any. They wrote about things which weren't real. Travelling in space, or between dimensions, or through time, all the most amazing stuff of the imagination, Uncle said."

"Let's take them," Elly said.

"Of course, I had no intention of leaving them here to rot!" Maia replied, scooping up several books onto one arm. "Uncle will be so excited! And the non fiction books will be an incredible addition to his library."

Elly picked up a book with the front cover torn, opening it to the first page.

"A million stars had passed this window," she read aloud, then stopped, looking at Maia. "How does a star pass a window? I don't get it. What a stupid book."

"It's not stupid, it's just from a different time. People liked this stuff back then."

"I guess things really have changed. Are you going to read them all?"

"Of course. You should try a few as well. A bit of escapism never hurt anybody."

"If you say so. I'll keep reading this one tonight. Maybe it gets better."

Chapter 23 – Familiar Places

At dawn, Maia and Elly left Ebeneezer behind, and made their way along Sackville Road. The glaring sun was warming, the dappled shade from the trees on the roadside gave bursts of visibility to the road ahead. Though she had never been here before, Maia started to feel like her destination was getting closer.

"It's starting to feel familiar," Maia said. "This place, it's starting to feel like Windsor."

"How far do you think we are?"

"I think we'll reach Windsor today," Maia replied.

Scarcely more than an hour had passed, when they arrived at an intersection, where an ancient green sign read "Wilberforce Rd", with an arrow pointing right, and beneath that, the words "Windsor" and "Sydney."

With a cheer, the girls turned right and followed Wilberforce Road, passing large, abandoned homes, and spacious open fields. Although the road was well travelled, some patches of the ancient tarred blue metal remained, and these had sharp edges.

They travelled with care, as the road wound its way towards its destination. After another hour, they followed the road onto a sturdy bridge. Though old, it was standing proud, and to the right, they could see the remnants of an older bridge this one had replaced.

"This must have been built late into the old times," Elly commented.

"Yes, and that's good for us. It's a strong bridge." Maia replied.

Across the bridge, they entered a built up area. Proud ancient stone buildings stood abandoned. Beyond a small intersection, in front of one of the buildings, was another old green sign. Maia drove them towards it.

The sign said "Windsor Road" at the top, indicating Paramatta and Sydney, followed by Macquarie Street, indicating Richmond and Penrith at the bottom. The sign had been repainted, probably many times.

"So we go straight?" Elly asked, seeing the word Windsor at the top.

"No," Maia replied. "Elly, we've made it, this is Windsor. Macquarie street is in Windsor. We turn right."

"How can this be Windsor? There's nobody here!"

"Trust me. This is what Windsor was in the old times. Now, the settlement is much smaller, but they repaint the signs, they still patrol the areas around it. This is Windsor, we made it."

"How far is your home?"

"That's," Maia paused, deflated. "That's still a long way. But I know the way, so it will be easier, knowing where to go. We need to stop here. I should inform them of what has happened."

They turned onto Macquarie Street, and continued into the main part of town. Before long, with the sun still not at it's mid day height, they arrived at a tall wall, constructed from old railway sleepers, with the words "Windsor Courts" painted on it. A tall steel gate barred their way.

"That's unusual," Maia said as she climbed down from the cart and approached it.

"Who goes there?" a man shouted from the other side.

"My name is Maia, I'm from Gospers village in the mountains. This is my friend, Elly, and our horses. I need to speak to the militia."

"Indeed you do," the man replied enigmatically. "They will be keen to see you."

The gate opened, and the guard watched outside furtively as the cart rattled through.

"You may leave your cart here. We will see to your horses. Your possessions will be safe with us."

"OK then," Maia said. "But why are the gates closed?"

"We have some friends of yours in custody. We have been ordered to tighten security until the trial is complete, in case there are other groups of bandits out there looking to free the men who abducted you."

"You have them in custody?" Maia gasped.

"Yes, with help from your friend Alex and a man from

your village, but if you can verify some things, the trial will go more in our favour."

"OK, I'll go to the militia now."

*   *   *

Artemis trotted along beside Alex, as they followed behind Greg. The older man marched with purpose, setting a hard pace to the long walk as they marched along the motorway.

"You're going so fast!" Alex said.

"We have a lot of lost time to make up. I promised Frank."

"I know you did. I promised Maia, but if Artemis collapses from exhaustion, she'll be angry with me."

"You'll drop before the dog, boy."

"You think so?"

"I know so," Greg said with a laugh. "That dog's got energy to burn. You're just some punk kid who thinks he can keep up with her. She's growing up fast, she won't be a pup for much longer."

"You think so?"

"They do a lot of growing in the first year. The rate we're going, she'll be just about in her adult body when she gets home. I was hoping to get her back to Maia before then."

"I'm worried. I noticed her nose is getting lighter."

"That'll be the nutrition. We're feeding her jerky, or whatever there is at hand. If it's not the right stuff, it will affect her pigment. At home, old Frank is strict with what he feeds them. He loves those dogs. He tells me about it all the time when we drink."

"I'm not making her sick am I?"

"No, boy. You're keeping her alive, just like you promised. But if you can give her some fresh meat a few times before you see Maia again, it might help her out."

"Like a rabbit? She loves those."

"They're good eating, if you're a dog..."

"They're good eating for people too, if you do it right," Alex said.

"I suppose they might be at that."

They stopped talking, walking in silence as they huffed up the hills and jogged down them. After a long day, they crested a rise and saw the bridge. The wind turbines turned lazily in the breeze, as workers tended to the pigs.

The guards at the gate watched as the trio approached.

"Where are you from, Travellers?" one of the men called out.

"I am Greg, I come from the village of Gospers, and I seek a girl who was abducted from our trade route."

"Then you had best come in, and speak to the elders. The boy and the dog can wait here."

Greg nodded, and walked through the opening gate, while Alex and Artemis remained behind. He walked the full length of the bridge, and then followed the guard beneath, and up inside the structure. He looked around, surprised by the extent of the settlement, until finally they arrived in a small room with an elderly woman seated at a long table.

"What is it?" the woman asked.

"This man claims to be from Gospers, and seeks the girl from there who was abducted. He is accompanied by a boy and a white dog."

"What is the dog's name?" the woman asked.

"Artemis," Greg replied. "She belongs to the girl I am looking for. I have promised her father I would see her delivered home safely."

"Then I am comfortable informing you she is no longer here. The girl and her friend have returned the way you came, to leave the motorway and travel to Windsor via Wisemans Ferry. I can have a map prepared, if you like?"

"I would appreciate that greatly," Greg said. "I also ask if we may stay here for the evening and continue our search in the morning?"

"That can be arranged," the woman said. "We can discuss with you, as an adult representative of Gospers, the arrangements for future trade we have already established with the girl pending her safe return to your village."

"Arrangements for trade?" Greg asked. "I guess the

girl has been busy taking advantage of her situation."

"Indeed she has, though the journey has not been easy for her."

*　　　*　　　*

"You are Maia, of Gospers village?" Daryl asked.

"Yes."

"What is the white pup's name?"

"Artemis. Have you seen her?"

"I have. She is with the boy, travelling with a man from your village at this time. What is the boy's name?"

"Alex."

"Then you must be Maia. I'm sorry, but I don't take any chances when a person claims to be a person of interest to the militia. If you saw the men who abducted you, could you confirm it is them?"

"Yes, I could."

"OK, and one other thing. Was there a man among them who tried to help you? Who tried to assist you in escaping?"

"Yes. His name was Barry."

"Good. I wanted to confirm his claim, and that of the witnesses. The rest of them don't know about him, but he is a former member of the Blackheath Militia, and a man I feel we can trust, if your testimony supports him. Would you be comfortable with his release?"

"I would. He is a good man at heart, far better than his companions."

"Thank you. I will make arrangements. For his companions, it will seem he escaped. That way if he needs to return to working undercover when the Blackheath Militia is once more active, he will still be able to do so."

"Then I will be careful not to reveal his secret."

"I am certain he would appreciate that. Now then, if you would come with me, we will have you identify the men, and then you may go. I am sure you are anxious to make your way home. One of my men will accompany you, of course, if you don't mind an escort to Gospers."

"An escort would be welcome," Maia said.

"Very good," Daryl said, standing and walking to the door. "This way, please."

He led her through the building to an area with sturdy steel doors, and approached one, sliding open a small hatch to look inside. He then turned to Maia.

"Please look inside. Was this man the leader?"

Maia did as she was asked, and then stepped away as Daryl closed the hatch again.

"Yes, they only called him Boss, but that is definitely him."

"Good. Then we can assume the rest of the men were his crew, thank you. You have confirmed what we need. These men will be tried and punished. You are free to leave when you are ready, but welcome to stay in Windsor as long as you need. We will have accommodation for you here in the courts should you need it."

"Thank you, I think I would very much like to leave straight away. It would be good to get home. But you mentioned you had seen Alex and Artemis? Where are they now?"

"They have returned in the direction of the Pacific Motorway, intent on following your trail. Which means they will likely return here, as you did, provided those along the way are agreeable to sharing news of your travels."

"Were they on foot?"

"Yes."

"Then they are likely to be many days before they return. By then I will be home. If you could direct them there when they return, I would be grateful. Although it would be wonderful to have Artemis returned to me, finding my way home has to be my priority now."

"Understood. I wish you safe travels. I will call for Harry, one of my men, to accompany you. He will meet you at the gates you would normally come into the courts from if coming from Gospers on a trade mission."

"Thank you."

*   *   *

Greg, Alex and Artemis set out at dawn from the bridge. Greg carried with him a signed agreement between himself and the elders regarding the future trade route, outlined exactly as they had agreed with Maia.

"Do you think we can catch up to her?" Alex asked.

"Likely not," Greg replied. "But all the same, I'll give it a good shot. She has horses and a cart, while we are walking. She also has a good head start, but since we have to return to Windsor anyway, we might as well follow her path. If she has run into any trouble, our arrival may be fortuitous. If we go directly to Windsor, and she has encountered difficulties, we won't be there to help."

"I agree with that plan," Alex said. "Just so long as she is OK, and we meet her eventually, it will be fine."

Chapter 24 – Going Home

With Harry, the escort, quick marching beside the cart, Maia and Elly made good time and enjoyed a safe journey into the mountains. Some sections were tricky with the cart, since the trail had only been maintained at a width to accommodate the smaller village cart and the dogs, but the horses managed well. Harry was invaluable at these times, hacking away at the vegetation to get them through.

After many days, they finally rounded the last bend, and approached Gosper's Village. It seemed quiet, but Maia soon caught sight of David and her father, working on one of the many fire breaks near the furthest flung homes. She waved, and her father beamed, waving back from a chair, his leg still bandaged, as David rushed to greet them.

"Maia! You made it back!" David shouted as he approached. "Have you seen my father?"

"No, but he left Windsor in pursuit of us several days ago. He'll be still a few days away as his path loops back to Windsor, and then home. He has a friend, and Artemis with him. I'm looking forward to them making it home."

"That's good news. Come on, I'll take you to your father."

"Why is he working? He needs to rest! His leg can't be fully healed yet."

"It isn't, but you try telling him that. It's not bad like it was. He can get around with his crutches. He's slow though."

Maia ran ahead of David, as her father begin to haul himself out of the chair, using crutches he had collected from the ground beside him. Harry, the escort, followed as David stared open mouthed at the horses, as though he had not noticed them before.

"Well, hello there," Elly said coyly.

"Oh, um, Hi," David replied.

"I'm Elly, Maia brought me home. I'm going to live here."

"Really?" David said, glancing around. "Well, welcome to Gospers."

"You're a shy one, aren't you?" Elly said, jumping down from the cart to face him, her eyes level with his chin.

"Um, no, I, um, I just wasn't expecting another girl..."

Elly laughed, grabbed his hand, and led him after the others.

"Come on then, I can tell I'm going to like you. You silly boy."

The group assembled around Frank, Maia rushing in to embrace her father. He returned the affectionate gesture, as Harry coughed.

"Sir," Harry said. "If I may have a word?"

"Of course, I'm Frank. I'm the trader for this village."

"My name is Harry. I'm a member of the Windsor Militia. I was asked to escort your daughter home."

"I thank you for protecting her," Frank replied.

"I doubt she needed much protection. She has been a busy girl on her journey, and thanks to her, we have apprehended a notorious group from the south. I hear she also has made a lot of progress building your trade routes to the east. If she is the daughter of a trader, then it all makes sense now."

"I am pleased to hear she has not wasted the experience," Frank said, "but I am far more pleased to see her home safe. There was a man seeking her, do you know of him?"

"He is safe and well, and likely several days behind us."

"That's good news as well. We will be needing his help on the breaks. And some of the water channels need attention he is well experienced with."

"Uncle can handle the channels," Maia said. "He designed them, remember?"

"Uncle can no longer help us with those," Frank said. "But it is best you speak with your mother. She is far better with such things than I."

"Why? What happened? What's wrong with Uncle?"

"Just talk to your mother. She will explain. Go to her, quickly now."

Maia ran, heading for the centre of the village. Realising something was very wrong, Elly followed. They reached the centre of the village, and Maia rushed to her family home and inside, Elly close on her heals. Her mother looked up from the table as she rushed into the kitchen.

"Mother!" Maia said, rushing to embrace the woman.

"Maia! Thank heavens you're safe!"

"Mother, dad said something about Uncle. What's happened?"

"Oh dear," Helen said. "I'm sorry, Maia, there was nothing we could do..."

"What?" Maia said, "No..."

The weight of her mothers silent tears shook her heart. It was as if she had been hit in the stomach. She felt herself buried by rocks of emotion, as she stood, shaking her head.

"No. No. It can't be, not Uncle." Maia screamed as she fled the house.

"Maia, Wait!" Helen cried, rushing after her daughter.

Elly, confused, and upset for her friend's distress, rushed after them. Maia turned and ran through the village, along the avenue of trees, and up to the door of the house where Uncle lived. The door was unlocked, and she rushed inside, calling for him.

As she ran from room to room, Helen and Elly entered the house and stood, neither sure what to say, as Maia rushed around, searching for her mentor. But he was nowhere to be seen.

"Where is he?" she cried.

"I'm sorry, Maia," Helen said. "It was about two weeks after you left. His cough was getting worse. His lungs..."

"No, it can't be. He told me it was nothing!"

"He passed one evening, in the square. He crawled down there, asking for help. He had a note, with instructions, telling us what to do. He knew he was dying..."

"No..."

"I'm sorry, Maia," Helen said, reaching to embrace her daughter.

"No!" Maia snapped, slapping her mother's arms away.

Maia looked around the room, which seemed so empty without him in it.

"No... Not Uncle."

The girl collapsed into her mother's arms and wept.

*   *   *

Frank waved as Harry left after refusing to accept the hospitality of the village. The Militia man insisted he had to return to make his report, and attend to his duties in Windsor. He promised a new patrol route would be established to Gospers, and that the militia would assist with the establishing of the new routes for trade Maia had worked to create.

Frank smiled. "She's certainly my daughter, that one. But this is much more than trade. She's got settlements working together. I couldn't have managed that. Perhaps things are going to improve."

"Frank," David said. "What's going to happen now?"

"I think what the girls have started, will be the forming of a new country."

"That sounds a bit much," David replied.

"Not at all. Windsor has fought to establish itself as a seat of government for decades, without success. But what Maia has done has seen them working together, negotiating with others, instead of lording over them. She's shown them that allowing trade routes that stay away from Windsor, protecting them, will get the militia greater respect. Over time, Windsor could become the capital of a small nation."

"Have you been drinking?"

"No, Son," Frank replied. "I would not be surprised if this was something Maia had in mind when she started negotiating with other settlements. Harry seemed to know a lot about it, she must have told him while he escorted them home. He said her abduction showed the militia they needed to do more than protect their own town, and the journey they took into the city helped them realise just how much more they could be doing. Without her, that change would not have occurred."

"If you say so."

"Just wait and see. It will be better for us if this goes the way I think it will."

*   *   *

"He said to give you this," Helen said, pointing to a wooden box on the table in the kitchen of Uncle's house.

"What is it?" Maia asked.

"Open it."

Maia did as her mother asked, and lifted the hinged lid on the box. A letter rested in it, on top of a selection of other items. The letter was in an envelope with her name written on the front in Uncle's familiar hand writing. Maia took it out and opened it, reading allowed.

"Maia, if you are reading this, my worst fears for myself have come to pass and I am now dead. I only hope you have returned to the village safely and without undue hardship. After you left, I searched but could find nothing to indicate where you had gone. I stayed late into the evenings. I perhaps should not have done. My health is taking a poor turn."

Maia paused, lowered the letter, and looked at her mother.

"It was my fault. He died because of me. If I hadn't gone missing..."

"That wasn't your fault," Elly snapped. "You were kidnapped. Keep reading."

"Maia, I'm sorry I never finished showing you everything there was to see. I would have liked to see you find horses. Perhaps you already did. Three days after you went missing, I found an owl. Remember I spoke of them to you? Well, it wasn't really an owl, it was a nightjar, a bird called a tawny frog mouth. But in the old days they were often confused for owls. Enough so that they are treated in stories as pretty much the same thing. They look like them, and even sound like them. It was in the forest not far from the village. So I found what I was looking for. I hope you did as well."

Maia looked at Elly, then her mother.

"I did find a lot, but I didn't want to lose him."

"It's OK, Maia, finish reading," Helen said.

"I have one more thing I need you to do for me, Maia. My family was originally from a place far to the east. There is an immense cemetery on the cliffs above the ocean, and we had a mausoleum there. My Sister and I interred our parents there when they died, and now, I need you to find her. My little sister, Wendy, will know where to take my ashes. It might take some time to find her, but she lives in a place called The Great Northern, with her husband and family."

Maia paused again, suddenly realising who he was telling her to find.

"Wendy, it couldn't be?" the girl gasped. "But I already found her!"

"There's more there, Maia!" Elly said, impatient to hear it.

"Once you have delivered my ashes, which are in the white jar in the box, if the villagers have followed my instructions, I ask you to return home, and live your days peacefully, teaching in my stead. My home is yours, along with everything it contains. Teach the children of the village well, Maia. Be the guardian of knowledge in this special place, as I can no longer be."

Chapter 25 – Sisters

Once her tears subsided, Maia made her way back to her parent's house. Helen had kept her room for her, exactly as it had been before she left. Maia felt wrong, to stay in Uncle's house, even if he bequeathed it to her. At least until he was at rest. Elly stayed quiet throughout, but close to Maia at all times.

"No," Frank said, as they sat down to dinner. "I understand that it is important to you, as it was to Uncle, but I will not allow you to take such a journey without company. Look at what happened the last time?"

"But dad, those men, they've been captured, they won't be out there."

"But others will. They moved north because too many of them were in the south. Others might do the same. And then there are the gangs in the city, I've heard stories, I don't want you putting yourself in that kind of danger again. It's not necessary."

"Dad, I have to get his ashes laid to rest. It's what he wanted."

"I know, Maia. And you will. But he has waited this long, he can wait a little longer. I can't come with you yet, but soon Greg will return. He has been travelling with the militia, he will have learned a lot about staying safe from them. I'll ask him to go with you."

"Then can Elly stay here, with us while we wait? I don't feel right making her stay at Uncle's on her own."

"Of course. But she'll have to share your room."

"I know, that will be fine."

"Then it's settled. You wait here. When Greg returns, you can take the ashes to the sea side, or whatever that place was."

"Thank you, Sir," Elly said. "I wasn't sure where to go."

"You're my sister now, remember?" Maia replied, with

a smile at the girl. "This is your home, as well as mine."

*   *   *

Greg and Alex walked with purpose, as they left Windsor again. The guard was quick to tell them Maia had been there, but they had already suspected it. Now it only remained to get to Gospers.

"Shouldn't you be headed home, son?" Greg asked.

"Not yet," Alex replied. "I promised Maia I would find her. Until I see her myself, I haven't fulfilled that promise. And I promised my mother I would make sure she was safe as well, and she'd be upset with me if I didn't. And I want to see Artemis home as well. I'm not one to abandon a task I've started."

"And you'll be wanting that horse back I suppose."

"My mother would like that, but even so, she gave the horse for Maia to escape without any real expectation of ever seeing it again. It was in the city to be sold, after all."

"Then I will see to it that the village pays for the horse. It will be a useful thing for us to have, especially with the new trade routes."

"I would be grateful for that. But I don't know how we will get payment to my mother. I'd like to stick around a while, if that's OK."

"Oh, You have that kind of interest in Maia then?"

Alex looked down, and mumbled.

"Only if she returns it. Does she have a boyfriend in the village?"

"She's rebuffed all the boys of Gospers, lad. If you think you have a chance of winning her affections, you had best speak to her father when we arrive, but if she rejects you, know that she has rejected all so far, and accept it."

"It would be awkward to stick around then, I suppose."

"Yes. But you will be a friend of Gospers Village for the rest of your days. You fought hard to save her, and to keep her safe. That will always be remembered."

*   *   *

Maia watched as several villagers erected a line of sturdy frames between the houses and the fields, in the place most exposed to sunlight. Nearby, the panels she had brought home from the bridge were neatly stacked, waiting to be installed.

It was heavy work, and it had taken several days to prepare enough wood, harvesting trees from strategic points in the nearby forest. As the last beam was secured in place, Maia heard an excited bark, and a boy's voice. She looked down towards the road into the village, and saw a glimpse of white in the distance.

"Artemis?" She whispered, then shouted as she ran. "Artemis! Come on girl! Come to me!"

On hearing her voice, the dog ran to her, leaving the boy and man behind as she rushed to her master. Maia knelt and caught the pup, now mostly grown, in her arms and wept as the dog licked her face in excitement. Maia held the dog for a long time, waiting for the others to arrive.

She stood slowly, keeping a hand on Artemis's shoulder as Alex and Greg finally approached. Maia grinned at them like an excited child, unable to conceal her joy at being reunited with Artemis.

"You kept your promise," Maia said, as her tears battled for freedom.

"Yes," Alex replied. "I brought her back. I'm sorry it took so long."

"Thank you," she said, taking a nervous step towards the boy.

"Maia, I..." He hesitated, looking down and shuffling his feet.

Greg laughed, slapped the boys back, and walked away.

"I'll go see your father, Maia. Look after this one for me, will you?"

"Maia, Um, would you..." Alex looked at her grinning, tear stained face, and his eyes darted down again, as his cheeks blushed crimson. "I'd like to stick around, if that's OK..."

"Alex!" Maia snapped, the rebuke in her voice forcing

his face up, to meet her eyes. "Don't be so silly."

He was crestfallen, as Elly approached. Maia turned to the girl.

"Wait a moment, Elly, This is important."

With that, Maia lunged into Alex, wrapping him in her arms and planting a kiss on his lips as her tears continued. The boy was stunned, and stood still for a moment, his eyes wide, until it finally hit him. She was welcoming him home, accepting him into her life as something more than a traveller or a friend. He slipped his arms around her, and finally returned the affection in her kiss with the fervour of his youth as Elly clapped and laughed for their happiness.

"Well now!" boomed Franks voice as Greg cackled, the pair approaching from the houses, Greg supporting his friend as he hobbled towards the tableau. "I think there is an introduction to be made here, but Greg has already spoken of your actions, Lad, and if Maia wishes for you to stay then you are most welcome in my home."

Alex broke away from the embrace, and turned to face Frank, thrusting a hand forward, he stammered in the most genuine way.

"I, I'm pleased to meet you, s s sir, My name is Alex. And I would very much like to spend some time with your daughter, if that is OK with you."

Frank laughed, his deep baritone chortle an unusual accompaniment to Greg's cackles. Maia looked at her father with a stern glare.

"I really don't think I have any say in that, Lad. Maia will do whatever she wants, her father be damned. She is the only one whose approval you need, and I think it is clear she has given it. Welcome home, Boy."

*   *   *

It was a week later, the street lights glowing in the misty mountain morning, and workers pushing a path through the trees as they commenced a new road to eventually link the village to the bridge, and other settlements in the area, in keeping with the plan Maia had settled with the other groups. A small group of Windsor

Militia men had arrived in that time, and were helping with the heavy work.

Elly and David hit it off, and they stood together, waving as the cart rattled out of Gospers. Elly had had enough travel for a while, and she was more than happy to settle in Gospers, leaving the adventures to others from now on. Maia, Alex and Greg rode in the cart as Barry pulled. They left Farrow behind, intent on giving Barry the slower travel needed to not over work the animal. Artemis stayed at home as well.

"Now, do you know where we are going?" Greg asked.

"Of course. The Great Northern Hotel. We have to give Wendy the sad news of her Brother's passing."

"Wait, Wendy? The Great Northern? Her brother?" Greg sputtered. "I knew we were taking Uncle's ashes somewhere, but I didn't bother asking more... Are you saying that woman is his sister?"

"Yes. Wendy at the Great Northern Hotel, who I spent some time with, is Uncle's sister. His instructions are to take his ashes to her, and then accompany her to their family mausoleum. Since Uncle never had children, I am the closest he has to do this task, as he and Wendy did for their parents."

"Well, no, I don't suppose he did have children. When he came to the village, he came with a partner who was strong and able, but sadly passed after a few short years. That was a man who could split a log! His arms were enormous, like trees. The opposite of Uncle. They came to own that house through his intellect and his partners muscle. Together, they brought the village out of a dark time and made it the happy place you grew up in. We owe a lot to both of those men."

"I wish I could have met him, Uncle's partner. Uncle never spoke to me of him, or why he had no wife. It wasn't important I guess."

"Uncle had love in his life, and moved on when that was gone. I suspect any talk of it would have been too painful for him though. But he loved you as his own daughter. I mean, he loved all the kids he taught, but you held a special place. You stayed on, you supported his efforts, you made it clear he was a valued member of our community. I think he needed that sometimes."

"So Uncle," Alex asked. "He wasn't from Gospers originally?"

"None of us are, if you go back far enough, Lad." Greg said. "That's why new comers are always welcomed. Because all of us are, somewhere in our family history."

"That's a very different outlook to some places," Maia said.

"Yes," Greg replied. "Like those tunnel gangs. But in time, the world will settle, and people will travel more freely again. You've started that process, with the new trade routes you made possible."

"But I didn't do anything, really."

"Sometimes, opening eyes to a possibility is as important as fighting back an army, or defeating a villain."

"If you say so."

*   *   *

After several days of uneventful travel, the cart rattled into the small courtyard in front of The Great Northern Hotel. Maia jumped down and grabbed uncle's box, opening the top and removing the urn. Hugging it close to her chest, she walked slowly towards the door as Wendy thrust it open and rushed out to meet her.

"Maia! You've returned! And I see you met your friends! This is wonderful news," the woman paused, looking at the girl, whose eyes were downcast, tears falling. "Maia? Maia, what is it?"

Maia raised the urn, and passed it to Wendy, whose eyes grew wide in understanding as Maia burst into tears.

"I'm sorry, Wendy. I'm so, so sorry."

Wendy took the urn and placed it on the table by the door and returned to sweep Maia into a motherly embrace, as she allowed her own eyes to leak the tears of a grieving sister. The pair stood for several minutes while Greg and Alex secured the cart and led Barry to water.

Finally, Wendy looked up, then turned, leading the weeping girl inside.

"Come inside, all of you. I'll fetch something to drink, I have some good tea, in honour of my dearest brother, who has gone to be with his lost love. He will be sorely missed, both here and afar."

Chapter 26 – Final Rest

Wendy and Maia left on horse back the next morning. Wendy fetched a large, ancient key from her room and after serving breakfast, instructed Alex and Greg to stay at the Great Northern until they returned.

"This is a personal matter, reserved for members of the family. Maia, as the one he requested carry this torch, is included as part of our family."

Maia sat in front of the older woman on Barry, as the horse trotted along the motorway. She held aloft a yellow flag, fluttering in the wind as they travelled.

"Why a yellow flag?" Maia asked

"In ancient times, a yellow flag was raised to indicate contagion. Later it was used to signify a death, regardless of the cause. When the old times came to an end, and the viruses swept through entire towns, the yellow flag became common once more, and they flew over many towns before they were destroyed. As things settled down, it returned to being the later meaning of a death in a neighbourhood, and is now used by people such as us, to signify a funeral journey, so that we may pass through the various gang territories unmolested. Even the tunnel gangs respect it. While we carry the flag, there and back, we will be permitted free passage to undertake the rights and burials required for our deceased family."

"I see. So there is a mutual respect for the dead among the various tribes that remain. It is a good sign, that at least one vestige of civilisation is still observed."

"There are many," Wendy said. "Sadly as has always been the case, what we have in common is greater than what separates us, but people focus often on the differences."

"The differences?"

"Yes. My brother used to be fascinated by the differences we ignore, but there are many we do not."

"The Differences we ignore," Maia mused. "I once asked him about skin."

"Skin?"

"In Gospers, as in Windsor, and the city, there are people of many tones of skin, some darker, some lighter, some pail as a cloud and others like charcoal, and everything in between. But we all exist together, and act as though it has no bearing on our value to each other, and signifies no difference in status or humanity."

"Yes," Wendy said. "That is how it should be. Our deeds reflect our value, and among those deeds is the valuing of all others."

"That's What Uncle said. But he told me, that in the old days, that wasn't the case. He told me, that people judged each other's worth as human beings based on the colour of their skin. He said the people of the world lived with conflict, distrust, and hatred for one another based on this kind of arbitrary judgement of each other, and it was sad that it took the end of times for us to finally change our ways."

"Sadly some of us will never learn. But those who do not learn this lesson are fewer in a world with fewer people and a hard fought for existence."

"What do you mean? Are there still people who judge others on their skin?"

"I fear there may always be, because there are always people who seek to elevate themselves above others. Being derogatory to a difference, however minor, is one way such people will always behave. Extending that derogatory nature into action, whether violent or political or economic, is one way humans have abused each other for millennia."

"I know that's true, I've seen the old records, the videos and things Uncle had, and it was so visible in some of those. But my heart breaks for our people, if what you say is true, and some of us will never change."

"The ones who never change, our only option for a future for all of us, is to deny them a voice. Do not let them drag others to their cause, instead drag them away from it. But there is no doubting they exist. They always will. What matters is what we do to prevent hatred from ruling our people as it once did."

They fell quiet for some time, as they rode on towards the city. As the ancient arches of the bridge over the harbour came into view, Maia looked up.

"That must be what happened to Elly."

"What do you mean?" Wendy replied.

"Oh, I was thinking about what you said, how some people never change. Elly was living peacefully, until some people came and murdered her family, and the others in her village, and stole what little they had. I wondered why anybody would do such a thing, but thinking back to the documents and videos from ancient times, that's the kind of behaviour people then used to do to each other, because of silly things like the colour of their skin or the language of their grandparents."

"Those kinds of people will, as I said, always exist. We must fight throughout our lives to silence them and stall their hatred," Wendy said with conviction. "Your friend Elly, Nigel mentioned her. She is the one you met at that settlement after you left my home, isn't she?"

"Yes."

They stopped on the centre of the bridge, the bright sun beating down upon them. As they looked out over the ancient harbour.

"It will be hard, but you should take her home, to that village. Whatever remains of it. Only when she is ready, of course."

"Why?"

"She needs to see it. The world will have reclaimed much of it, and time will have healed the scars of the land. Seeing that is important to healing the scars in her soul. If you don't do that, those scars can foster new hatred, and a desire for retribution against those who have wronged us. The way forward, to a brighter future for us all, is to remove the hate from our lives, because that hate is one of the things, I believe, that led to the fall of our ancient civilisation."

"You remind me of Uncle."

"Consider this his last lesson," Wendy said, smiling

sadly. "Understanding the way to a better future is the gift that studying the past gives us. My brother wanted that brighter future more than anybody."

"I want it too."

"We all do. And we honour his legacy by seeking it. What will you do?"

"I want my village to become more than it is. I want it to prosper, and trade with more settlements, exchange knowledge, reawaken this land by bringing all the many people together. No more conflict. Peace and happiness for all of us."

"You already started, didn't you?"

"What do you mean?"

"My Brother loved your village. I never quite understood why. But he chose that place over all others. And then he chose you, to continue his work. You have created a new connection, between my home and yours, as his connection fades away. You have created other new connections, I believe."

"The bridge," Maia mused.

"You visited there, didn't you?"

"Yes, after I left your place, I went there. I discussed trade with them, and we agreed to build a new road between my village and them."

"A new road? That's ambitious. There hasn't been a new road in a century."

"Windsor have already sent us workers to help."

"You have Windsor helping build links between settlements that aren't Windsor?"

Wendy shook her head as she started the horse moving again. She smiled as they left the bridge, and looked down at the girl in front of her.

"You really have set about changing the world, haven't you? You honour my brother's memory in greater ways than I. I look forward to your brighter world."

*   *   *

As the sun set behind them, Maia and Wendy arrived at a long stone wall. It ran to the peak of a hill, where enormous gates stood open. They rode through, and Wendy stopped, then dismounted, before helping Maia down as well. The land sloped away down hill, towards the ocean, and graves in their thousands looked out to sea.

Taking the urn, Wendy led the way through the cemetery. In some places, grasses and weeds grew tall, in others grave sites were clean and maintained as families continued to visit.

"The cycle of life and death still goes on here," Maia said as she followed Wendy along a crumbling concrete path.

"It always will," Wendy said. "Whatever comes to pass, even should nature one day reclaim this place, the memories of humanity will always reside in these hills, in these crumbling plots of land, with their stone and concrete monuments to a people long departed."

Wendy led the way to a small stone hut, with an enormous rusted steal door on one end. She handed Maia the urn, and stepped up to the door. Taking out the old key, she unlocked the door, and wrestled it open.

"I visit here once each year," Wendy said. "It has been a while since my brother did the same. I feel he was always here in some piece of his heart. He wept for days when we brought our parents for their final visit."

"He rarely spoke of them to me," Maia said. "It seemed to pain him if it ever came up."

"They never approved of some of his choices. But they loved him unimpeded regardless. There was one regret he held, and that was not clearing the air with them on a single matter. That was something of a loss for him. Especially after he lost his beloved. Come, it's time for him to rest. All will be at peace for him at last as he joins them."

Maia followed Wendy inside the tiny mausoleum. Shelves lined the walls, dozens of urns resting there, the dust of ages lightly settled. Wendy took a cloth from a pocket and began to dust a space on the shelf, beside an urn which matched the one in Maia's hands.

Wendy gently brushed the dust from the urn on the shelf.

"Hello, old friend," Wendy whispered. "I come with sad news for us, but perhaps happy news for you. You are to be reunited with my brother at long last. May you rest together in death, as some would not allow you to rest together in life."

She turned, took the urn from Maia, and placed it gently on the shelf beside it's twin. Wiping away a tear, Maia laid a hand on Wendy's arm, as the woman wept openly, powerful sobs erupting from her throat as she fell to her knees.

"Was that Uncles...?"

"Yes, he was my dear friend, and Uncle's one great love. We grew up together, the three of us. But now, now they both have gone on ahead of me. One day my children will place my urn here, beside my brother's. And one day my husband will join me, and then years from now my own children. And in time, we will all be forgotten except by those who come to visit."

"I will visit this place. As often as I am able, if I may."

"You may of course," Wendy said, scooping Maia into a warm embrace. "You have a place here as well, if you choose to accept it. You are the closest to a child my brother ever had, and he considered you as such. You are a part of my family now, if not by blood, by demonstration. The key to this place will be ever at my hotel, and you will forever have a room there. My brother is at rest now, and he will be here, waiting for your stories of his legacy, and of how you have taken his dream forward in his stead."

Chapter 27 – Change

Maia wiped her eyes as she walked from her bedroom in the big house she had inherited from Uncle. It was the first day of spring, according to the calendar of the old times, and was a little more than a year since she had laid her mentor to rest.

Artemis wandered by her side, keen for her morning meal and a chance to relieve herself in the garden. She knocked on the door of another room, one Uncle had used only for storage when he lived there.

"Elly, I'm going to make tea. It's time to get up, there'll be carts arriving this morning from the bridge. And Alex and David will be back from the trade run to Windsor later today."

Maia walked into the kitchen, and placed the old electric kettle on the bench, a sturdy stone slab she had Alex buy in Windsor on his last trip, and place across the old fireplace Uncle had cooked on for decades. Plugging it into the outlet she had fitted to the wall, Maia smiled, grateful as ever for the solar panels and batteries she had brought back from the bridge.

Each home had one outlet initially, and they used the electricity sparingly, but she had word from Alex on the new telegraph that they had secured more panels and extra batteries with this trade mission.

Alex was bringing old friends as well, and Maia wanted Elly to be ready when they arrived. Neither girl had seen the boys from Wisemans Ferry since their return to Gospers.

As the morning sun shone through the glass skylight Maia had fitted to the ceiling of the kitchen, she fetched cups and a tea pot, and soon had hot beverages in hand, walking from the kitchen as Elly came to the door.

"What project do you have in mind for the boys this week?" Elly asked, used to Maia's often complicated plans for the young men when they brought home new equipment.

"With Nico's help, I think the boys will have no trouble building an electric kiln for making bricks. There's a large clay deposit the bridge people are considering making use of, and I hope to trade for clay with them, to make bricks to build some better homes for people in the village. Stone is so hard to move and work with over such rough terrain, but clay can be made to bricks of any size or shape we want."

"You're always ambitious. Do you think they can produce enough power to do it?"

"With Nico, I'm sure they can. I've arranged a turbine for the task from a settlement north of the bridge, and I'm hoping Nico can fit it to a tower, like the ones in Wisemans Ferry."

Maia poured the tea into the cups, and passed one to Elly as she walked to the back door, opening it to allow Artemis outside. Following the dog, the girls walked around the side, and to the front of the house.

In the distance, the villagers were already active, with several people from Windsor and other towns also wandering around in the morning sun, going about business with the people of Gospers as though it wasn't unusual.

"There are so many people here now," Elly said.

"Yes, I never dreamed Gospers would become such a busy place. They've already improved the roads in the village, from the tracks they were before, and that new road out of the mountains has sped up trade to Windsor like I never dreamed."

"And the other one, towards the bridge. There are so many settlements out that way I never heard about. They're all benefiting from what you started."

"It's nothing on what the ancients built, but we have to be careful. This area was set aside as precious wilderness, even by the most vandal ridden governments of the old times. We have to ensure we allow nature to exist beside us. As Gospers grows, I worry what damage we might be doing."

"But nature has taken back so much of the city. Do you think it will be a big problem?"

"Perhaps for our grand children. We have to put limits on the numbers to live here, so that they resettle to places humanity already destroyed. I would hate for something like the city to be built on the legacy of Gospers. That's why I agreed for Windsor to negotiate to become a capital for our little nation. It's central and surrounded by settled lands. And they have shown themselves to be immensely useful to us so far."

"I hope it's all as good as you wish," Elly said. "Not all people are as good as you might think."

"That's why we will be bringing in rules about who gets to lead and how. Only those with the vision, the decency and the ethics to lead us to the future Uncle wanted will be permitted to do so. They have to understand our past, so they can lead us to our future. I'd hate for another downfall, we might never recover from it."

"Do you think Windsor will agree to that?"

"They will. They live with the reminders of the fall all around them, we're spared that scenery here in the mountains. Windsor will do whatever it takes to avoid a repeat of history."

As they watched the tree lined trail to the house, a cart rattled onto it from the village square, Hugh standing on the front, waving his hand high and smiling as he saw the girls near the house.

"That'll be my turbine," Maia said, rushing down the drive, in order to direct the cart to a different location.

Artemis ran after her, yipping happily as her master ran, Elly following at a walk behind them, then breaking into a run as she saw Alex and David's trade cart pull up behind Hugh's, piled high with goods from Windsor.

A third cart came behind them. Maia looked for a long, perplexed time until she recognised the woman driving it. She smiled, and rushed to welcome Alex's mother, before directing the three carts to their proper destinations. It was going to be a busy spring trading season.